DARE ENHANCED EDITION

THE PIXIELAND DIARIES BOOK 3

CHRISTINA BAUER

COPYRIGHT

Monster House Books
Newton, MA 02434
ISBN 9781946677808
First Edition

**For All Those Who Kick Ass, Take Names,
and Read Books**

CONTENTS

AUTHOR'S NOTE

$\mathcal{D}$ear Reader,

Sometimes a story wants a lot of breathing room. In other instances, the tale is done with fewer pages. DARE falls in the latter category. Over the years, I've learned not to fight with a book that does—or does not—want to end.

As a thank you for enjoying this shorter reading experience, I've included a bonus appendix of exclusive goodies. I hope you enjoy every word.

Best wishes,

CB

PREFACE

*Our story begins with a log written by two pirate adventurers:
Calla (age nine) and Dare (age ten).*

CALLA'S & DARE'S AWESOME PIRATE LOG ABOUT HUNTING DOWN THE OGHAM SWORD

Beware!

These are the chronicles of the mighty pixie, Calla, and the amazing elf prince, Dare. We are pirates searching for hidden treasure in Faerie. No gold coins for us (Dare has tons already.) Instead, we want a magical weapon called the Ogham sword. Why? You can tap things with it and magically change them. Who wouldn't want that? Therefore, both of us pinky-swear to find the weapon before Calla's 10th birthday and Dare's 11th.

Since we're such expert pirates, the sword is basically ours. Here's how we'll use it:

- Calla will poke the Elven High Council and change

them into nice people. Right now, they're all big meanies who don't like pranks for some reason.

- Calla will also set all the human changelings free.

- Dare plans to turn some squirrels into ice leopards. This is a good idea. There are way too many squirrels in the forest behind his palace and ice leopards *roar out* snowstorms. Talk about awesome.

OTHER FAE: Don't read this log if you have droopy ears or cockeyed wings. Our adventures are so exciting, some loose stuff might fall right off you.

You are warned.

About Me

*H*ere's how I, Calla, started this adventure.

Everything happens because I live inside an acorn along with my parents, Poppa and Muti. One day, I'm playing around with my fairy dust magic when I make up a new spell…

Mini drum bunnies!

(This comes back to pirate treasure soon, I swear.)

Back to the bunnies.

I create these little furry sweeties who hop and smash their heads together. They make a good beat. But I guess having a few hundred jumping around in our acorn is a little too much for Poppa and Muti. My parents are tree sprites and really, really, REALLY old. Imagine two tiny people with big heads, cute wings, and lots of wrinkles. That's Poppa and Muti.

My parents ask me to "get out of the tree for a while." They say this a lot. I promise to help Bilge at the Pixieland Citadel (after I get rid of the mini drum bunnies). Bilge is a chatty hobgoblin with green skin and sideways ears. He has a piggy familiar named Oinky.

Soon I fly off for the citadel. Once I get there, Bilge asks me to sweep up the basement. This is where our pirate adventure really begins. It's in the basement where I find a secret pirate scroll called…

The Legend of the Ogham sword

I read the whole thing three times. The Ogham is a weird blade that shows up once in a kazillion-million years. Even crazier, it grows *inside* a magical oak. There's also a guy in the tree trunk who protects the sword. He's the Root Knight.

Now the scroll gets to some really good stuff. Once you find the Ogham tree, you place your palm against the bark and say these magic words.

Root Knight, Root Knight

Holding your magic inside this tree
Root Knight, Root Knight
Open and give your sword to me

The oak then splits apart to reveal the Root Knight inside. The tree guy gives you the sword.

And here's when the magic happens.

Let's say you want to change a squirrel into an ice leopard. You gently tap your blade against the squirrel and say:

Magic of plenty

And—*POOF*—the squirrel becomes an ice leopard. Fun!

Dare and I vow to find the Ogham sword. Dare's my best friend and a winter elf prince. He lives in a palace instead of an acorn and has a butler who makes "ice cream cones." Only they aren't really ice cream because Dare's mother thinks that stuff is sugary garbage, so the butler uses fruit. And there's no cone because that's also bad for you. Which means they're really just fruit bowls, but Dare and I pretend they're ice cream. It's strange.

Back To Our Treasure Hunt

The pirate scroll also has a drawing of the Root Knight. I will copy it onto the next page. The knight has a back-up lady who helps him out, but she's not in the picture for some reason.

Root Knight & Ogham Sword

DARE

alla is cool. She draws really good pictures.

Calla wants us to be pirates. I think that's great. We're hunting down the Ogham sword. I go into my royal library and look for clues. Turns out, the last person to find the sword is an elf named the Usurper.

I don't find any pictures of the Usurper, though. That's too bad. Calla could draw it for our pirate log.

DARE

oday, Calla and I walk around the woods behind the palace and look for the Ogham sword. We touch different pine trees and say the magic words.

Root Knight, Root Knight
Holding your magic inside this tree
Root Knight, Root Knight
Open and give your sword to me

We don't find the Ogham sword… but my servants do start looking at us funny. Mother is convinced that everyone's worried because I'm eating too much sugar and raising baby snow sharks in my bathtub. So I promise to only eat fruit bowls from now on.

But the baby snow sharks are totally staying.

This morning, I sneak into Bilge's witchy workroom and get caught. Bilge makes me write, *it's called a potion master's study, not a witchy workroom* four hundred times.

Bilge can get so crabby about nothing.

After I write my punishment, I explain to Bilge how I need ingredients for a spell to find the Ogham sword. I also say how I'll use the sword to free human changelings and make the Elven High Council less snippy. And I also-ALSO add in Dare's idea with squirrels and ice leopards, only I explain how *I think* Dare should ask for *baby* ice leopards because they'd be cuter... but that's really Dare's call when it's his turn with the sword.

It's a good speech, but Bilge gets all screechy and says

that finding the Ogham sword is a terrible idea. I guess the weapon's really dangerous. According to Bilge, if you want to turn a squirrel into an ice leopard, then you tap it with the Ogham and say:

> *One for many,*
> *Magic of plenty.*
> *Make me ice leopards!*

Only it won't just change one squirrel. All squirrels everywhere would turn into ice leopards. That could get messy.

Bilge and I go back and forth for a while. Finally, I agree to *think about* dropping the Ogham sword as our ultimate treasure. Bilge says I'm a handful and goes off for some "me-time" in his ~~witchy workroom~~ potion master's study.

With Bilge gone, I snoop around and find a new book that actually shows the Usurper. Dare likes it when I draw. ~~And I like it when he smiles. My stomach gets all woozy and everything.~~

I'll copy that picture onto the next page.

Usurper

DARE 

Calla shows me her Usurper drawing and tells me what really happens when he wields the Ogham sword.

Not good.

Calla and I talk about it for a long time. We decide that we'll just find the sword and put it somewhere safe.

This afternoon, Bilge catches me and Dare "borrowing" a magical compass from his potion master's study. Actually, it's Oinky who finds us. Dare and I get so caught up, we forget to feed the piggy his lunch. Never mess with Oinky and mealtime.

Once more, I explain to Bilge how Dare and I need the compass in order to find the Ogham sword and stop the Usurper. Uh oh. The second I blab about the Ogham, I want to shove the words back in my mouth. Bilge lost his mind when I talked about the sword before. Bringing it up again is just dumb.

Bilge narrows his little button eyes, which means he's totally scheming. Dare and I are about to make a run for it when Bilge says he'll tell us a tall tale. There's no way we're leaving now. Both Dare and I love story time, even though I think Bilge sometimes uses it to talk us into stuff.

Anyway, Bilge tells us about the Usurper and the Ogham sword...

Bilge's Story

There's a blade called the Ogham sword which can magically change things. Most fae can cast spells, so they really don't care about this weapon. But there's one elf named the Usurper. He's a null, which means he's born without magic. The Usurper wants the sword.

Here I point out that the Usurper's parents should have named him Fred or something. Nothing good happens if you call your baby the Usurper. Bilge and Dare agree.

Back to the story.

The Usurper hates having a crappy name and no magic. If this meanie elf ever gets his hands on the Ogham, then he'll use it to change everyone into something new. Only it won't be ice leopards... it will be a pile of bones.

Dare and I gasp at this part.

But when the sword finally appears, the Usurper is foiled by some very smart fae and he never gets to use the weapon and destroy all of Faerie.

The end.

It's a good tale, but Bilge ruins it by saying that the whole thing is a myth (which is a grown-up word for *lie*.) Next Bilge says that Dare and I should start a new log where we look for the real Errigal instead of the fake Ogham sword. It's a cool idea. The Errigal are summer realm outlaws who rob from rich elves to help poor fae.

Dare likes the idea of finding the Errigal. I'm not so sure.

Then Bilge promises to cast us ice cream cones if we stop searching for the Ogham sword. Both Dare and I really like that idea.

There's only so long you can pretend that *fruit soup* isn't weird.

DARE

This is the official last entry in *Calla's & Dare's Awesome Pirate Log About Hunting Down The Ogham sword.*

The search is over.

PS. I just ate nineteen ice cream cones. Oinky helped.

DARE

Our story continues when Calla is sixteen and Dare is seventeen. Last night, they shared their first kiss...

After fighting a gargoyle king...

Calla becoming Queen of the Summer Fae...

And both of them saving Calla's father, King Tristan.

That pretty much brings you up to speed from the last two diaries.

DAY 95

*D*ear Diary,

    This morning, I wake up with a plan. Brace for the drumroll…

    Ba ba ba ba ba BAAAAAAA!

    And here it is…

    Now that I'm Queen of the Summer Fae, I shall flush some seriously crappy stuff out of my realm. And because this diary will surely become a major historical document, I will list the two poopy things in question.

My Massive, Idealistic, And Yet Totally Achievable Goals As Queen

    One. Free the human changelings who are trapped in Faerie.

Two. Make the Elven High Council accept *all* fae as co-rulers, not just those of the *snooty and pointy-eared* variety.

Together, I call this my Changeling-Council Plan. These two things have been my main obsession for years, ~~so long as you don't count Prince Dare~~.

Which brings me to the present moment. I lie curled under the covers in my royal bedroom (which is totally pink and cute) and consider my next move. There are lots of folks I should consult about my Changeling-Council Plan. But there's only one person who never-not-once questioned that I'd eventually kick the council's butt and redefine changeling-hood.

Prince Dare.

Keeping a diary means being brutally honest. Here goes. There's a secret goal on my previous list of queenly stuff.

Three. Dare and me.

I don't have anything more specific at this point. What can I say? I'm only sixteen.

But I do know what I need from Dare in terms of my Changeling-Council Plan. After all, the guy grew up in the winter court. He can advise me how to get stuff done. And the fact that Dare lives half-way across Faerie isn't a problem, either. The prince and I have a secret way of contacting each other that's worked since we were kids: we appear to each other as ghosts.

So it should be easy to ghost-talk with Dare about my Changeling-Council Plan.

It isn't, though.

I have two big issues. First, I've got a supernatural and ticklish feeling crawling up my back. And when I say *ethereal tickle,* you think *impending doom.* The last time I got this sensation, the Fartburger Trolls launched a surprise attack on Pixieland. I stopped them with a prank, but it was still a close call.

The second problem is far more serious. I cannot, not, NOT be the first one to ghost-call the prince.

Why? Last night, Dare and I went on a sleigh ride and totally smooched. Although it was my first kiss, I know the rules. Dare must begin contact with moi, not the other way around.

So instead of getting ghosty, I shall spend my morning drawing something that is completely unrelated to Dare.

Like a tree.

Dare

I miscalculated.

For some reason, I drew how intense-n-cute Dare looked right before he kissed me for the first time.

Better try again.

Courtship Rings

*O*ops.

Those are the matching rings Dare and I now sport for our magical courtship.

In my defense, the rings did change their appearance last night. By the time the prince dropped me off at the palace, the bands had gone from looking like twisty cords of silver into solid loops of bronze. That's what you call a supernatural transformation.

It's only natural to draw that kind of thing.

Maybe.

Possibly.

Ugh. Who am I kidding?

This has nothing to do with kisses or courtship rings. I'm just avoiding the reality that being queen is overwhelming and my willpower is toast. Plus, that ticklish feeling is getting steadily worse.

I'm definitely contacting Dare.

That said, ghost-chats must take place once a girl reaches the height of her regal cuteness. It takes me a few tries—okay, six—but eventually, I cast a spell for the right winter outfit. After all, I'm visiting Dare in his snow-bound palace. Ghost Me can't feel the cold, but there's a fashion principle involved.

My final outfit will undoubtedly be important for future human movies about my life, so I'll list it below.

My Adorable Wintry Ensemble

Pants. I end up with the leggings look. Pink, of course.

Jacket. This is a cropped number with a big hood. I wear it over a matching turtleneck.

Boots. These are oversized with puffy pink fur that does not exist in nature, even in Faerie.

Mittens. Pink. Furry. Perfect.

Overall, I think this ensemble highlights my tall-ish stature, pink hair, and violet eyes. Good job, me.

Once I'm dressed and ready, it's time to contact Dare. The ghost magic is easy to activate. First, I pull off a mitten and expose the thin scar on my palm. Dare has a matching line. As my second and final step, I speak into my hand.

"We daren't go a-hunting," I state.

This is a code phrase between us. It's from a human poem.

> *Up the airy mountain,*
> *Down the rushy glen,*
> *We daren't go a-hunting*
> *For fear of little men*

Which means I'd like to chat about nothing major. If the prince is ready to talk, then my scar will pulse with white light.

Which it does. *Yay!*

Now things get tricky. Ghost-talking is a lot like carrying on two conversations at once. My physical body stays here in my sweet pink bedroom, but my ghostly self goes wherever Dare is in the winter castle. As long as I stay calm, no one but the prince can detect my presence.

An electric charge fills the air. White sparkles swirl around me. The spell begins. Little by little, the world around me turns semi-transparent. At the same time, another scene overlays my bedroom...

The hearth room of the Winter Palace.

This is a small wooden space used for secret royal chats. Heavy tapestries cover the walls. Four bulky wooden chairs are positioned in a semicircle around the blazing fireplace. On the far-left seat, there sits Saita. She's Dare's mother and the positive definition of *ice queen*. I'm talking high cheekbones, piercing eyes, and an all-white wardrobe.

I've seen her so many times over the years, I could draw Saita from memory.

As a matter of fact, I think I will.

Saita

Saita stays in the far-left chair; Dare remains parked in the far-right seat. Today the prince is dressed in what I call his *winter royal casual* look. That means Dare wears heavy leathers, massive boots, and lots of knives. The style works on him, considering how the prince has that rugged elf thing going on. He's all strong bone structure, major muscles, scruffy beard… you get the idea.

I sashay across the room and take the seat next to Saita. Once settled, I kick my legs out and cross my furry boots at the ankle. Dare doesn't look at my fashion creation directly, but the wisp of a smile rounds his mouth.

No doubt about it. The prince totally approves of my new footwear. Fluffy pink boots for the win!

As usual, Saita can't tell that I've entered the room. *Heh heh heh.* This part of *ghost talking* never gets old.

Dare leans forward, resting his elbows on his knees. "I'm sure you don't plan to sit silently forever, Saita."

"Correct."

"Then?"

Saita smacks her lips, which is a sure sign she's about to drop a major verbal bomb. "What are Calla's goals as queen?"

Boom!

Saita's question short-circuits my brain for a minute. Dare shoots the barest glance in my direction. His gaze reminds me to provide some kind of answer.

I straighten in my chair. When I next speak, I use a more regal tone. "As Queen of the Summer Fae, I shall free the changelings and redo the Elven High Council."

That totally sounded good. I must work 'shall' into more of my royal sentences. It's a reflex to glance over to Dare's mother for a reaction.

But Saita can't hear me. Again.

And I enjoy that fact immensely. Again.

Dare relates the plan. He does a great job, even including the 'shall' part.

Saita flares her nostrils while thinning her mouth. That's the same face she made when she discovered how

I gave legs to all her garden slugs. I was seven at the time.

"Oh, no." Saita waves her hand dismissively. "Those goals are massive, idealistic, and totally unachievable."

I roll my eyes. "Folks always say that. Is everyone stuck in a mind-control spell?" Here I speak in a snotty voice, just because I can. "That's totally unachievable."

Saita frowns. "Did you hear someone?"

I pop my hands over my mouth. If I get too worked up over something, then I become audible.

For his part, Dare is mister smooth. "I detect nothing. Please continue, Mother."

Like always, Saita buys Dare's BS without question. It's like when Dare was ten and said that ice sharks make great pets. Saita bought the whole story.

"Let me put it this way," continues Saita. "Calla's a sweet girl. Over the years, I've come to see her as my—"

"Daughter?" I offer.

"Pet," finishes Saita. "Like a mongrel puppy who keeps coming around for hand-outs."

"What the hell?!" I cry. At the same time, Dare pretends to have a coughing fit. If I got emotional before, then I'm definitely cranked up now. And Dare's covering up for me, the sweetie.

"Are you alright, son?"

I mime zipping my mouth shut and Dare stops

hacking up a lung. "I'm fine. The air is rather dry in here."

Saita sighs. "I know you've gotten attached to the girl." She gestures toward the courtship ring on Dare's hand.

"Girl? Calla is a *queen*, mother."

"Please," continues Saita. "You're seventeen. She's sixteen. That's far too young for a committed relationship. You never would've started this magical courtship if I hadn't tried stopping you that day."

Which is true. I wanted Dare to notice me, not swap major jewelry. But Saita didn't want Dare joining the Save Calla's Dad Extravaganza. The Winter Queen tried to magically force the prince to stay home. And I really needed Dare's help in order to rescue my father. So the prince started our enchanted courtship and beat out Saita's powers. Long story short, Dare helped me to free Dad. In the end, that's what's important.

"I pressed you too hard back then," adds Saita. "It was a mistake. But now, you must tell Calla to forget about changing anything regarding the summer realm."

I roll my eyes. "Fat chance."

Dare tries to hide a smirk, but he doesn't work too hard. "I'll see what I can do."

"Good." Saita marches out the door without saying another word. She does that sometimes.

The prince and I are left standing and staring at each other. Silence presses in around us. I try to think of something witty to say, but I come up with zero. Saita's *mongrel comment* stays stuck in my head, blocking out any other thoughts.

Dare moves closer. "I'm sorry about Mother. She has trouble adjusting to me growing up, let alone you."

I hug my elbows. "Saita's always been a little extreme."

He gives me a crooked smile. "A little?" He steps even closer. "Are you okay?"

"Yes… Maybe… No." I throw up my hands. "It's a big deal being queen. I'm totally faking my way through this. What if Saita's correct? Maybe I shouldn't change anything that Protector Lazare did."

Dare tilts his head while pursing his lips. It's one of his *thinking faces*. "I've an idea. How about we take a day off?"

That grabs my attention and how. I've spent years imagining Dare asking me out on dates. And here it is, actually happening. My mind drains of all thought. It's a major effort to ask a single question.

"When?"

"Let's say tomorrow. I'll fly my sleigh over to the summer palace and we can leave for another adventure."

Some part of my consciousness pokes at my brain,

hoping for a coherent comeback. Still nothing. At last, I get out two words.

"Oh, okay."

Dare inches even closer. When the prince next speaks, his voice sounds exceedingly husky. "Let's say 10 am?"

"Sure. Yes. Cool."

"Perfect."

I raise my hand, ready to speak the incantation that will end our ghost chat. A memory appears, stopping me.

"Oh, I forgot. I promised to see Ivy tomorrow."

This is a huge deal. Ivy's my new friend and fellow summer fae. I don't have a ton of buddies who are my age and gender. Actually, Ivy is it. And she's a sweetie. Case in point: Ivy helped me get ready for my first date with Dare. And I promised her post-smooch details (which have yet to be delivered). There's no way I can leave my only girlfriend hanging.

"How about we meet up the day after?" I offer.

Dare gives me one of those smiles where his eyes sparkle. "Definitely."

"Until then." I speak into my palm. "End the spell."

With that, an electric sense of magic presses in once more. Fresh white sparkles fill the air. The study chamber fades away while my own bedroom comes back into full focus. A weight of worry settles on my shoulders as I consider my next regal move.

Queening is hard.

Pacing the floor, I plot the next step in my Changeling-Council Plan. How can I actually decree anything that my subjects will follow? As it is, my nobles won't even visit the castle. How can I expect them to set changelings free… or allow new folks onto the High Council?

These are big problems, and I have zero answers. So I spend the rest of my day in the royal library, reading up on royal decrees while ignoring the ticklish sensation along my back.

Something bad is definitely coming my way.

It can get in line.

- Calla

*D*ear Diary,

It's Ivy day!

When I wake up, I'm super excited for some girl-time with my friend. Sadly, I still have that ticklish feeling. Whatever's coming, it remains en route.

Once I'm dressed and ready, I take off to find Ivy. She works in the palace, so there's a short list of places where my friend could be. In the end, I find her hanging by the unicorn stables.

(Yes, I have a royal collection of unicorns. Total job bonus.)

Ivy stands behind a wooden partition. Just seeing her from a distance lifts my heart. My friend is all things spritely and happy, what with her wide blue eyes, springy blonde hair, and bright smile. Her dresses are always woven through with living greenery.

As I step closer, it's clear that Ivy's talking to a very tall elf with long black hair and skin the color of cocoa. No question who this guy is: Vadin. He's my unicorn wrangler

(Yes, I have one of those, too).

Vadin whispers something in Ivy's ear. Probably a lot of stuff about how excited he is that I'm the new queen.

I wave. "Hey, there!"

"Oh!" Ivy yelps as she jumps away from Vadin. I freeze.

Vadin wasn't whispering to Ivy. They were kissing.

What a mistake. It's not like Ivy knew it was "her day with me" or anything. My bad. I assumed Ivy would just be sitting around, waiting for her queen to show up and chat.

Awkward!

I take a big step backward. "Crap timing. Sorry about that."

Ivy and Vadin rush forward. "Don't go," says Ivy. "You haven't officially met Vadin."

This isn't exactly true. I'm the kind of girl who puts 'meet your unicorn wrangler' high on my *to do list* as queen. Still, I suppose another official introduction wouldn't hurt.

"Good morning," I declare.

"Greetings, your Majesty." Vadin bows so low, I'm surprised he doesn't fall over. He rises and smiles. "It's great to meet you."

Ivy bounces on the balls of her feet. "I'm so excited this is happening." She focuses on me. "Did you come by to talk?"

"Well, since you asked…" I begin.

At this point, I could certainly blab about kissing Dare, but that really isn't a Vadin-friendly conversation. So I move on to other, more regal topics.

"I'd love to tell you both about my new royal decrees," I announce.

Not sure what I expected to happen next. Some genuflecting, maybe. Lots of wide-eyed awe, definitely.

That's not what happens.

Ivy elbows Vadin in the ribs. "Did you hear that? Decrees! I told you, she's always playing pranks."

It's a reflex to pull on my ear. *Maybe I didn't hear that right.* Ivy can't possibly think that I'm kidding about actually ruling my own kingdom.

Vadin beams. "Your pranks are legend across Faerie. I can't believe I'm witnessing one in person!"

I fold my arms over my chest. Maybe a change in body language will make me look more regal. "I'm serious. I want to end the practice of stealing humans and making them changelings. I also plan to make the High Council represent everyone in Faerie."

Ivy giggles. "Right. You're *so* seriously thinking about ruling." She and Vadin twiddle their fingers together. It's a mix of holding hands and tickling palms. Which would be sweet if they weren't laughing at the very idea of me doing my job.

This conversation really isn't going toward a positive place, so I decide to change the subject.

"Have either of you sensed anything terrible coming?" I ask. "I mean, to our world. Faerie."

Ivy throws up her hands. "And she pulls another one!"

Vadin chuckles. "We're so scared!"

Ivy beams. "I count three pranks now."

With that, it's official. *Time to retreat.*

"Great to meet you, Vadin. See you both later."

And I haul ass back to my bedroom. Once I'm cuddled under my comforter pile, I indulge in a rare activity: feeling sorry for myself. Yesterday, Saita called me a mongrel pet. Today, Ivy and Vadin think I'm nothing but a prankster.

This shouldn't get to me.

It totally does.

I end up drawing a picture of Buttons, the mushroom fae who lived near the home tree where I grew up.

Buttons never questioned my ability to do anything. Although, to be fair, Buttons could only gesture toward the horizon and say, "view, halloo!"

In this moment, that counts as a major endorsement. I'm drawing the guy.

- Calla

Buttons

Dear Diary,

After my close encounter with Saita, I've a tough time falling sleep. Waking up is no picnic, either. In fact, it isn't until high-pitched voices echo in through my window that I finally open my eyes. A single thought reverberates through my mind.

The guards are at it again.

I rise from bed, pull on my velvet robe—the one with *Queen Calla* written on the back, naturally—and saunter over to my balcony. The Buttercup Forest spreads out below. It's an undulating sheet of yellow leaves that stretch to the horizon. Guards in gold armor race under the canopy. A few even run smack into each other, they're so flipped out.

I'd be shocked, but Dare's coming. The guards do this every time the prince visits.

I cup my hand by my mouth. "Captain Solei!"

Since this is a major historical document, it's important to note that Captain Solei once arrested me on behalf of Protector Lazare. At first, I asked her to run my guard just so I could watch her squirm. Now, she's growing on me.

Sure enough, Captain Solei marches to stand under my balcony. "Good morning, your Majesty." She looks the same as the other summer elves, namely tall, lithe and gorgeous. It's her voice is what sets her apart. Solei sounds like she's smoked about a metric ton of human cigarettes.

"Report out," I command.

"We've received a magical alert. An intruder flies toward us."

"Is it someone from the winter realm who's driving a sleigh, perhaps?"

"Correct."

Growing up, it used to make me crazy how Bilge would ask me a million questions instead of just telling me what he thought. Now that I'm a ruler, I get where my old hobgoblin buddy was coming from. People must think before they act. Just listening to me order Solei around won't help the synapses fire in her brain.

"And who could be flying this way?" I ask.

Solei tilts her head. "It's probably Prince Dare."

"And is that a problem?"

"Why, no. He's your, uh…"

"We're officially courting."

"But we don't *really* know if it's him."

I could hate myself for asking more questions, but I don't. "And how could you find that out?"

"I suppose we could use the magical spyglass and check."

"And if the spyglass shows that it *is* Dare?"

No answer. Not a shock. It's amazing Solei lasted this long with independent thought.

I continue. "If it *is* Dare, then you don't need to panic. So, how about you get everyone back information while you use the spyglass?"

"Yes, your Majesty." Solei salutes once more before stomping off into the forest. There's a guard station nearby that holds all their supplies.

I shake my head. *Honestly.* The smallest thing happens and the palace guard freaks out. Ivy says they're used to taking cues from Protector Lazare… and the dude lost his mind over everything. I can believe that.

With the guard situation sorted out, I get myself ready for some Dare time. After some contemplation, I decide to go with my classic pink dress, conjure up a breakfast of Pixie-Os, and watch the skies.

Now, I've spent a little time with humans. I know they have traditions about winter elves and sleighs. In their version, an overweight old guy drives a clunky red wheelbarrow. Totally wrong. You haven't lived until you've seen Dare tool through the sky in a sleek blue sleigh driven by four thoroughbred reindeer.

Ah well. Just one of the many reasons why it sucks to be human.

As Dare closes in, a golden sphere rolls out from under my bed. This is Sammy the scepter. Think about a magical atomic bomb with the personality of a puppy, and that's Sammy. He holds all the inherited power of my role as ruler. I love him to pieces.

Right now, Sammy's in his orb shape as he bounces around my bedroom. No question what all the excitement is about, either. Everyone in the palace is terrified of Sammy. And with good reason. After all, the power of the scepter is what exploded Protector Lazare.

Still, all that fear makes for a very lonely Sammy. When my buddy Oinky is around, then the pig and Sammy jump around and have a great time in general. Yet when there's no Oinky? The reindeer make for great playmates.

Which is why Sammy's now careening around my

bedroom. He even knocks over my favorite portrait (the one where I'm riding a unicorn.) That said, I can't be crabby. Sammy needs his fun-time, too.

Dare soars down from the heavens to float-park just outside my balcony. He's in his *outerwear mode* today—a look that involves a heavy fur cloak and extra-long swords. The prince scans the ground nearby.

"No one threw javelins at me this time."

As conversation starters go, this isn't too odd. The guards usually try to knock Dare out of the sky.

"Oh, I had a talk with Solei," I explain. "I'm encouraging her to use magical reconnaissance versus going right to panic mode."

"That's a shame. I enjoy the flight practice."

"I know, but the guards are really noisy when they freak out."

Dare grins. "Understood." He looks me over from head to toe. "You look perfect."

I twirl around. "Oh, this? It's just my regular pink minidress."

"Which is my favorite." He extends his arm in my direction. "Shall we?"

I take his hand. As always, Dare's skin feels all things warm and firm. An electric charge of connection erupts wherever we touch. Our fingers entwine as I step onto the sleigh. Dare begins to pull me closer when it happens.

Sammy arrives.

My magical ball-o-drama decides that now is a great time to boing right into me, Dare, and the sleigh. Sammy then takes to bouncing between the reindeers' antlers. The animals love it, by the way. It's like human volleyball, only with magic, golden orbs, and reindeer.

I can't help but laugh. Sure, Sammy just busted up a possibly romantic moment, but there's no denying that he's a little round ball of awesome. I take my typical spot on the sleigh's front bench. "So what's the plan for today?"

Dare sits down beside me. "I could tell you were feeling blue, so I did a little snooping around. I've discovered something rather important."

I squirm on the bench. This will be good. "Tell, tell."

"Right now, the Errigal are in the Talking Desert."

I gasp. "Wow."

The Errigal are a renegade group of summer fae outlaws who rob from rich elves to help the poor fae. Their location of their renegade camp is a big secret. Dare and I have been trying to find them since we were kids.

Captain Solei calls up from under the sleigh. "I couldn't help but overhear what the prince said, your

Majesty. If you're considering visiting the Errigal, then I must point out that it's very dangerous. They hate the summer throne."

"Don't worry," I call down. "They hated Protector Lazare. The Errigal don't even know me. It'll be fine."

That's what I say. What I mean is that Dare and I are always rushing off into danger. It's what we do.

I look to the prince. "Ready?"

Dare flicks the reins. "Let's fly."

The reindeer take off. Within seconds, wind roars in my ears as we soar over the Buttercup Forest. My heart beats at double speed. Dare and I have imagined this adventure many times when we were kids. Now, it's really happening. I lean against Dare's shoulder and enjoy the journey.

It's over too soon. The Talking Desert is a short flight from the palace. Minutes later, Dare lowers the sleigh to land on a flat stretch of crimson desert. Columns of red stone loom all around.

Dare and I step down from the sleigh. My body feels light as air. This is another personal goal of mine that's now achieved in a big way.

Visiting the Talking Desert.

And as places to visit, this one's a sight to record. So that's what I'll do on the next page.

Talking Desert

Dare and I walk between the red pillars of stone. Meanwhile, Sammy keeps playing antler-soccer. Dry air bites into my lungs. Sand strings my eyes.

Cracking noises sound. At first, I think the red columns are going to fall over.

Then I realize the truth.

The stones are turning into faces complete with slits for mouths and dark holes of eyes. And they begin to sing.

"Hello... hello... hello!"

I always expected The talking Desert to be filled with chatter. But the song stuff is cool. The music reminds me of something between smashing rocks and a barber-shop quartet.

I wave. "Hey, there."

Dare bows slightly at the waist. "Greetings."

"We see you," sing the stones. "Run!"

The ground shakes. Bits of rock tumble from the columns. What looks like red dragons race out across the sand. Some are plump and stout. Others are lean and wiry. As they get closer, it's clear that none of these creatures have wings. These aren't dragons.

They're fire drakes.

Which means they breathe out geysers of red-hot flame, but can't fly. On a fear scale of one to ten, I'd give them an eleven.

In such situations, Dare is really the expert. After all, he's the one who kept snow sharks as pets.

"Should we worry?" I ask.

"No, they're just scouts. They won't hurt us."

The earth rumbles more fiercely as the fire drakes array around us. Then they all stop in place. The world falls silent once more.

I must admit, that's a nice move from the fire drakes. I wish my own guards could be that coordinated.

The biggest drake leaps up into the air. That's really something to see. His blood-red scales are mixed with some golden hues. That marks him as their king, or what the fire drakes call their vizier.

My heart beats at double speed. This is my first time

meeting any fire drake, let alone the vizier. Sure, there are a few fire drakes that align themselves to the summer court. Sadly, these creatures are all super old. None of them can even breathe fire anymore. None of them have visited the summer palace. I haven't expected them to show up.

At this point, I should probably stand still and stay quiet. But that's not really a queenly move. So I go with a casual greeting.

"Hello, everyone. I'm Calla."

The vizier jumps up again. This time he spits out an arc of fire into the air. It's pretty impressive, not to mention something that induces a combination of fear and sweat. And it's a sight worth remembering. I'll add a drawing of it.

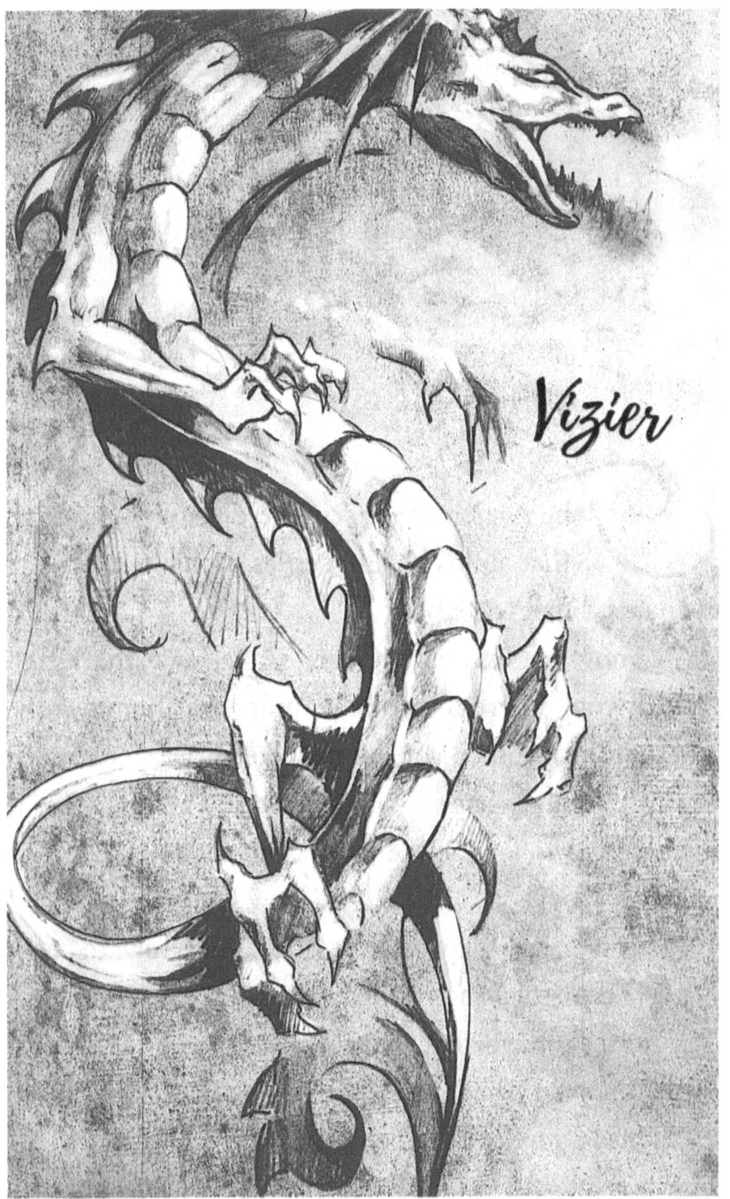
Vizier

The vizier lands corkscrew-style—meaning that all his weight settles on his tail. I didn't even know that was a *thing*.

"I know who you are, Queen Calla," says the vizier. "And if you're here to bring us under the thumb of the summer throne, then you are mistaken."

I lift both my hands, palms forward. "Oh, no. This is just a *hello tour*. One totally independent ruler to another."

This seems to help in terms of attitudes towards moi. The vizier then swings his massive head to glare at Dare. The prince returns that angry stare with one of his own.

Not good. I decide to step in.

"This is Dare," I offer.

The vizier sniffs. "I know who you are. The Winter Prince."

My eyes widen as I realize the problem here. Unlike the fire drakes, all ice dragons submit to Saita's rule. Not that they show up in court or anything. So the vizier is worried that Dare wants to extend his empire.

The sniffing and glaring keeps going. To be honest, it's getting a little boring, so I step in again.

"Guess what?" I ask. "I'm about to decree that the Elven High Council will become the Everybody Council. I've heard you keep lots of different folks here in Errigal. How about a tour?"

The vizier takes in another deep inhale. "That scents of the truth."

I shoot the prince the side-eye. "What's with the sniffing?"

"Fire drakes have highly-developed senses of smell."

"Huh." Learn something new every day and all that. I refocus on the vizier. "So how about that tour?"

"Is there nothing else you wish?" asks the vizier.

"Nope, just a tour," I reply.

"What she said," adds Dare.

The vizier does a final inhale. "Another truth." He shakes his head. "I'd been expecting another lie."

"I don't blame you," I state. "Lazare wanted to

execute you all for treason, considering how you stole some of his stuff."

"Stole?" asks the vizier. Smoke curls from his nostrils. This isn't going well.

"I mean, you reappropriated some royal gold. Anyway, Lazare was a creep. For all you know, I could be a total nut job, too. You're wise to be cautious."

The Vizier grins. This is something to see, considering how the expression stretches along the fire drake's entire jawline. "How about I give you a tour of the Talking Desert instead of our main encampment?"

"Love it," I state.

The drake army scuttles away in a cloud of dust and noisy claws. Dare and I walk around with the vizier. I ask a ton of questions. The vizier tells me all about the many kinds of fae in Errigal. Each group has its own leader. We picnic on the top of a rock pillar while the desert sings about friendship and sunshine.

The day flies by. All too soon it's time for me and Dare to climb back into the sleigh. The vizier towers over us and smiles.

"Perhaps you both can return one day," offers the fire drake.

"We'd like that," says Dare.

"When you come back, perhaps you'll meet our other

groups and their rulers. Maybe even have an audience with the secret one who leads us all."

"I'd really like that," I say.

Beside me, Dare grins. "Same here."

Both of us would love to meet the Errigal's secret head honcho. It's another one of our adventurer goals from when we were kids.

The vizier tilts his mighty head. "And what do you think of Dare's true purpose today?"

I do a double-take. "True what?"

"Shall I tell her or will you?" asks the vizier.

Dare takes both my hands in his. "I wanted you to see what it's like to have many groups and leaders. Everyone here has a voice. We only met the vizier for the fire drakes, but that's just one type of fae. There are dozens in the Errigal."

Rustling sounds fill the silent desert. Looking about, I see faces pop out from behind all the many columns and boulders. There are creatures everywhere. Some sit atop pillars. Others lurk inside rock crevices. I spy naiads and trolls, flower sprites and orcs… even elves and ice dragons.

I gasp. They must have been watching us the whole time.

Dare gives my hands a gentle squeeze. "See? This is a

small example of your large vision for the Everyone Council. It's working for them. These fae are happy. You can bring that to your entire realm. Don't give up."

"My magic could sense the prince's true purpose, " says the vizier. "The prince is right. Your cause is just." He nibbles his lower lip. "Only, we were wondering…"

After that sweet speech, I'd give Dare and the vizier just about anything. "Wondering what?"

"Would you pull up a ley line for us? We've never seen it before." The vizier lowers his voice. "We've met summer elves in the past, but never one like you."

Ley lines are the magical cords that connect Earth and Faerie, as well as time and space. My birth mother is the Ley Queen, which means she's the only person can manipulate this power. A ley elemental.

I'm just starting to learn all this stuff. Un til recently, I didn't even know we were called ley elementals. That said, I do know enough to put on a show for the Errigal.

I raise my arms. "And now, I shall pull a ley line from the ground!"

Everyone gasps. It's awesome.

Closing my eyes, I reach out with my senses. Some places have lots of ley magic. Other spots? Not so much. Fortunately, this area is heavy with power.

I step forward a few yards, stopping where the

energy is strongest. Kneeling, I rest my palms against the sand. Then I press my fingertips into the ground.

The ley line buzzes with cool energy just below the surface. I wrap my fingers around the magical cord and pull upward. The glowing line pulses with blue energy.

I raise my voice for the crowd. "If I wanted to see Earth, I would twist this line into a door shape. It would then become a portal to another realm."

Everyone gasps again. It's just as cool as the first time.

I drop the ley line. "Show's over, guys."

There are cheers and applause. Unlike the mongrel-time with Saita, I'm having fun.

Together, Dare and I step back into the sleigh and take off. The reindeer really make for a great exit. During the ride home, I cuddle into Dare's side. We decide to take the scenic route back. By the time we return to the summer palace, the sky's pockmarked with stars.

Dare stops the sleigh so it hovers by my balcony. I lock gazes with the prince. "I don't know how to thank you for today."

Dare leans in and brushes the gentlest kiss across my lips. "There's one way you can show your appreciation. Make your dream happen. I want to be there when you announce those decrees."

I let my wings unfurl. But at this point, I don't need them to fly. I soar back into my room and start contemplating how to make my Changeling-Council Plan come to life. And I reach a major decision.

Sometimes, all you need is one person.

- Calla

*D*ear Diary,

This morning, I wake up to a cold sensation across my palm. It's Dare. He's using our ghost spell connection.

I whisper into my palm. "What's up?"

"I need you."

Dare only says that when it's two things: Saita and trouble. The ticklish sensation on my back returns with a vengeance.

"I'll be right there," I reply.

I get ready in record time and activate the contact spell between us. Within minutes, I'm Ghost Calla once more. And I'm back in the hearth chamber of Dare's castle.

As I suspected, Saita is here as well.

Both Dare and Saita are parked in their regular seats around the fireplace, so I return to my old chair as well. Once settled, I scan the faces around me. Dare's features look tight with worry. Saita grips the armrests of her chair so tightly, she could snap the heavy furniture into bits. I've seen that white-knuckled thing before on Saita—it only happens when she's really upset.

This time, Dare's mother starts the conversation without any prompting.

"I heard a rumor from our servants," says Saita. "They've been speaking to their counterparts at the summer palace. Calla claims to be planning some major decrees. The servants think it's a joke. Is it?"

"No," says Dare.

"You must stop her from causing trouble. There are threats at work here that could destroy all of Faerie."

Dare and I exchange a dry look. There's a reason we secretly call his mother Chicken Saita. The woman has two modes: No big deal… and *run for your lives!*

Saita stands. "Lazare knew about the risk. That's why he planned to keep everything the same."

Now it's Dare's turn to rise. "With all of Faerie at risk, aren't there better means for protection… other than muzzling Calla?"

It's weird being the only one sitting, so I stand, too.

And I give Dare a big thumbs-up on the *other than muzzling Calla* line. That's some solid support.

"I don't know what you mean," whispers Saita. Dare's mom always talks in a low voice when she's lying her head off.

"We should pull in *allies*," clarifies Dare.

As if Saita doesn't know.

This is an ongoing fight between these two. Dare wants to find out the identity of his biological father. Saita's like a vault on that one.

"Knowing your father? What a ridiculous idea!" Saita speeds out the door. It's another one of her classic moves. The woman always exits the room when she's about to lose an argument.

Dare and I are alone.

"Saita can be needlessly harsh," he states. "I hope she isn't too much for you."

All of which is Dare's way of asking a single question: *Will I stop my decrees for the summer elves?*

"Let me put it this way," I state. "Last night, I came up with a brilliant idea. Three words: magically-binding decrees. Lazare has an old wizard study that's located somewhere in the palace. I'll redo it into my witchy workroom, cast the decrees and make everyone do the right thing."

My answer: *not a chance.*

Dare moves closer. "Will you look through Lazare's study before rebuilding it into your own workroom?"

"Uh huh." My eyes widen as I see where Dare is going with this. "I like the way you think."

And kiss. Although now isn't the time to add that part out loud.

As it happens, I don't need to say a thing. Dare gives me one of his intense stares. He knows I'm thinking about smooching, the smarty pants. He gives me a sexy side-eye and keeps talking.

"From what Mother said, Lazare knew there was a possible threat to all of Faerie. Perhaps we can search around his old study together and check for clues."

"I'm in." And Maybe I go on tiptoe a little, just in case Dare wants to kiss me or something.

The prince steps away. "Please understand. Mother can be easily excited, but this is different. And you've been getting premonitions lately."

As if in response, the sensation on my back turns so intense, it's as if I'm being prodded with a thousand needles at once. "What do you mean?"

Dare fixes me with one of his most intense stares ever. "I must be clear before we go forward. I firmly believe that this mystery threat is dire. Do you really want to explore it with me?"

I nibble my lip. I know why dare is asking this question. My mental plate has been overflowing these days. "What do you think is the risk here?"

"Mother said Faerie could end. I believe her."

Which means this is a big decision. So I make two lists. One for ignoring the threat. And another for fighting.

Why I Should Ignore This Mysterious Doom

One. I have a lot going on.

Two. No one thinks I can cast two little decrees, why would I think I can help prevent the end of Faerie?

Three. That's really it for this list.

Reasons To Track Down This Catastrophe And Punch It In The Throat

One. I could die.

Two. Dare could die.

Three. Everyone could die.

Four. Fighting bad stuff is just what I do.

And that settles it.

I let out a long breath. "I may not be able to stop whatever this disaster is, but I won't give up."

Dare bends over, wraps his arms around my knees,

and lifts me up extra high. I rest my hands on his shoulders and stare down into his beloved face.

"What's this for?" I ask.

"You've made the right choice, but I suspect you're wondering if you're up to the challenge."

I wince. "Maybe a little."

"This is to remind you how tall you are to *me*."

I smile from ear to ear. "And who else really matters?"

Dare winks. "Exactly my point."

Little by little, Dare allows me to slide down his body. I sense every line and muscle along the way. My mini journey ends with my feet on the ground and our mouths in a kiss.

We spend a lot of time together after that. And there are some things even my diary doesn't need to know.

- Calla

DAY 99

*D*ear Diary,

Witchy workroom day!

Today Dare and I visited Lazare's old wizard workroom in the Summer Palace. It's not like the location is some big hidden mystery.

All you have to do is follow the smell.

Some small voice in the back of my head says I should feel really somber at this moment. After all, Lazare had my job not too long ago. We've both ruled the same kingdom. Sure, Lazare had his issues, but doesn't everyone miss at being their best self? And in the end, all life is precious.

And I do feel a twinge of grief at the idea of stepping into a place where someone else just lived and worked.

Or maybe that's the ticklish dread feeling that's still working its way down on my spine.

Tough call.

Turning back to the sad moment. Lazare's life is a total tragedy. Even so, there are also some very good reasons why I'm not crying snot strings onto Dare's shoulder right now.

Why Protector Lazare Kinda-Sorta Had it Coming

One. He not only abducted humans from earth, he sold them to other nobles.

Two. Lazare tried to kill my father.

Three. If Lazare had just handed me Sammy the Scepter to me—*like he should've in the first place*—then the evil protector wouldn't have gotten himself blown up.

That's a pretty good list. Also, it turns out that it's hard to feel too mopey when I'm holding Dare's hand.

All in all, I'm feeling mighty chipper as Dare and I march through the hallways of the summer palace.

Correction. *My* summer palace.

As we close in on Lazare's old wizard study, the smell of rotting fish gets worse. No wonder the staff avoid this spot. I'm ready to dry heave and we still have a few hallways to go.

At last we reach the door. It's a heavy iron number

with round rivets along the edges. We open the slide-style handle and look inside.

Eew, just eew.

Why Protector Lazare Is Way Piggier Than Oinky

One. Trash everywhere. I'm talking smashed boxes, crinkled wrappers, and broken bottles.

Two. Everything seems to be covered in a thin layer of rotten eggs. Like a Cobb salad blew up in here.

Three. Lazare also seems to have collected fish heads for some reason. There are a number of stacks towering around the room. Also, he could've cast a spell to stop them from decaying, but he didn't. Lazare is really odd.

When Dare and I next speak, we sound like we've got stuffed-up noses. In truth, we're just talking through our mouths. At this point, it's a survival tactic.

"Cleaning spell?" I ask.

"Yub," says dare. He really means yup, but I get why it came out strangely.

I cast my spell with pink tendrils of faerie dust. Dare summons little tornadoes of ice. Both magical entities eat through the layers of food and trash. Not gonna lie. This is some heavy-duty gunk. It feels like hours slog by as we pump more energy into our castings.

Finally, we can see the very top of gray stone walls

that lie beyond the piles of garbage. The bit of a mega doorway comes into view.

Wow. So there's another door in this chamber that was hidden by all the stink and goop.

Lazare, you tricky guy.

I point to the mostly-hidden entrance. "Bet you a magic wand that Lazare put all this junk in here to keep everyone away from that door."

"Agreed." Dare points to a break in the trash. "See that?"

And I do.

"Looks like Lazare had an underground—or rather under-*trash*—path to the door."

"It's clever." Dare tilts his head. "Not sure why Lazare didn't just cast a spell, though. However, the fellow was rather unusual."

Scrunching up my face, I refocus my energy and spell. Before, it was all could do to just not puke. Now I can't wait to get enough trash out of the way to see what's behind that door. All in all, this garbage room is acting like warding spell. The stench keeps folks away.

Which leads to a big question: *what's behind that door?*

It must be his *real* sorcerer's study.

More hours slowly tick by before we've cleaned up enough of the garbage (and the stink) to make our assault on the now not-so-hidden entrance.

And since this is another historical moment, I shall now draw a picture of the door.

Lazare's Secret Door

*L*azare's secret door is a little rusty. It takes a few tries, but Dare and I eventually pull it open enough to enter the chamber beyond.

The place is totally empty.

Unlike the last room, the walls here are all smooth and yellow. The scent of grease hangs in the air.

Not what I expected.

Dare gestures to a spot by the door. "See that?"

A big red button sits smack dab in the middle of the wall.

"Oh, we are so hitting that button."

Dare chuckles. "Ladies first."

"No, you discovered it. You do the honors."

This is an old rule between us. Whoever finds the treasure chest gets to open it. That's just pirate manners.

Dare steps over and hits the button. Everything goes bonkers.

Wall panels appear and flip around to reveal mannequin versions of elves. The same happens with the floor. Tiles slide aside to allow more mannequins to rise. And they all start talking at once.

When I went to earth, I saw some video of a place called Disney. There were fake pirates who sang and did other stuff. What's happening now reminds me a lot of that.

Only, instead of pirates, it's elves.

there's a lot of overlapping chatter, but I do catch a few phrases.

"You're the greatest sorcerer."

"No one casts better spells than Lazare!"

"Hey, there, you powerful magic guy you."

Wow. Of all the secret things I thought Lazare might be up to, this didn't make the list. At all.

"What is this?" asks Dare.

"I think I know. Give me a minute." I set my pinkies in the corner of my mouth and whistle. In short order, a golden ball bounces into the room. It's Sammy, my magical scepter.

I grin. "Hey, buddy."

Sammy bounces up to land in my hand. Once there,

he takes his regular shape. Basically, he looks like a hunk of golden tubing.

"Sammy," I begin. "You used to be wielded by Lazare."

The scepter goes limp as a wet noodle in my hand. "Ha, ha. I'll take that as a yes." Sammy goes back to his regular shape. "Other than when he wielded you, could Lazare cast any magic at all?"

Sammy goes back to his limp mode. "In this case, I'll take that to mean, *no, Lazare couldn't cast a thing on his own.*"

Sammy melts from my hand and onto the floor. After that, he retakes his golden ball shape and bounces his way out of the room.

I look to Dare. "That's another *yes* from Sammy."

Dare shakes his head. "I can't believe it. Lazare was a magical null."

"I caught him hiding Sammy inside the folds of his robes. He must have used the scepter for even the most minor of spells."

Dare nods. "Which explains why the outer room was such a mess. Lazare couldn't cast a spell to keep folks away."

I lean back on my heels and scan the room of mechanical mannequins. "And it was all so he could come in here and pretend to be a sorcerer."

Dare steps slowly around the room. "Lazare must have used Sammy for at least some of the magic in here. These mannequins seem to be saying things their living counterparts actually spoke to Lazare."

"How do you know?"

"I found me." Dare moves through the mechanical crowd. Sure enough, there's a fake version of Dare. The nose is smushed in and his hair is totally a wig. But there's no avoiding the resemblance.

"I won't marry your daughter," says Fake Dare.

I'm so shocked, my eyes almost bug out of my head. "Dang. That spell really recorded the last thing you said to Lazare." I scan the room, looking for a mannequin of me.

No such luck.

Not that I care.

Okay, I do care a little bit. Over the years, I really took time to irritate Lazare. There was that one time where Lazare was being a mega-creep, so I have him diarrhea and a long wait for the bathroom. You'd think he'd put at least one version of me saying how much I like him.

However, I do find a mannequin version of Saita. What her faked-up double says is worth the fact that Lazare skipped over me.

It's a total shocker.

"Tell me about the Ogham sword, Lazare. I know it's about to destroy all of Faerie."

Every inch of my body feels like it's put on ice. Except for my back, that is. My spine feels so ticklish, I want to scream. This is the threat that's hanging over my people.

The Ogham sword.

I crook my finger at Dare. "Uh. Over here?" Grinning, the prince steps to my side. "What is it?"

The moment Dare hears fake Saita's words, the prince's mouth falls open with surprise. "Oh, no."

"Remember that weapon from when we were kids?" I ask.

"The Ogham sword," says Dare. "How could I forget? The Usurper tried to find the sword once. He planned to use it to destroy all of Faerie."

I smack my lips. "Looking back, Bilge was totally fishy about that whole thing."

"True," adds Dare. "Why would a hobgoblin be the only guy to have serious details about the Ogham sword? No one else even knew it existed."

"Well, I know what I'm doing tomorrow: going to the Pixieland Citadel and chatting up Bilge."

"And I'll have another talk with Saita. Maybe if I drop the name Usurper a few times, she'll share more of the full story." He inspects the room. "For now, we should listen to what all the other figures say."

"Good idea. Maybe there are more clues."

We spend hours listening to the mannequins. A few talk about bribes. Many ask for a good price on their next human changeling. Every time I hear that, it makes me so angry, I could scream. I want to cast my enchanted decrees and fast. But that can't happen until I have my witchy workshop. And that chamber can't get created until my spells are done cleaning out this place. Magical spaces work better if there's a base of power beneath them.

Which means the discovery of this chamber is a minor bummer. Clearly, Lazare didn't have any magic, so he could never leave magical residue behind to help with my new witchy workroom.

What a bummer. Still, I always felt a certain zing of power by this place. I'd like to keep my new witchy workroom here. I just have more stuff to clean up before I get started.

Oh, well. Finding out that Lazare is a magical null? It's still totally worth it. And the cleaning spells that Dare and I pumped into this place will leave some energy behind. So there's that.

In the end, it's a long day but a good one. By the time we finish up, both Dare and I are exhausted. The prince heads back to the winter palace. I pace my bedroom and try to process this latest news.

The Ogham sword is back.

Soon, the Usurper will return as well.

As potential disasters go, this is a doozie

With every passing moment, more nervous energy zings through my limbs. I can't wait to visit Bilge tomorrow.

With any luck, I'll get all the answers I need.

- Calla

ear Diary,

Today I fly over to the Pixieland Citadel first thing in the morning. For me, that's 10 am.

I do my normal entrance. That means using fairy dust to shrink down in size and slip through a window. Bilge would usually be waiting in the reception chamber.

He's not. The place seems empty. I fly upstairs to check his potion master's study.

Still no Bilge.

Although my hobgoblin buddy is gone, I still make a major discovery. The potion master's study itself is the revelation.

I've been helping out Bilge since I was a kid. This room is prepped for a major brewing. Oak barrels line the study floor. All of them are empty, which means Bilge will soon fill them with ingredients. My friend is either brewing a small amount of complex potion, or a huge amount of something basic.

Which one is it?

There's no way to answer that question yet. That said, it's clear where Bilge is right now. He's off somewhere getting the ingredients he needs. That never takes more than a day or so. If I come back tomorrow, Bilge will probably be back.

Which leaves me in Pixieland without a Bilge to cross-examine.

An image appears in my mind. It's the drawing of Buttons that I made a few days ago. I made it to remind myself how someone believes in me, even if the person in question can only say, "view, halloo."

Now I realize my mistake. You know who always thinks I'm awesome, even when I fill their acorn with mini drum bunnies?

My parents.

I'm not talking about the people who genetically made me. That would be the Ley Queen and King Tristan, who are hanging out together in Mom's castle and having a second honeymoon. Nope. I'm talking about Poppa and Muti, the amazing tree sprites who raised me. And I can't forget Jolly, the naiad who lives inside the mega oak that was my childhood home.

Next stop: Poppa and Muti.

With the decision made, I fly off toward the hill that I call home. It doesn't take long to get there. I soar across my lands, making a straight line for the familiar hill where Jolly should stand.

Only there's nothing here. I flit around in a circle, scanning the scene in every direction.

Is this the right spot? Yes.

Is my Jolly here? No.

An electric sense of panic streams through my body. I cup my hand by my mouth. "Jolly? Jolly!"

To my right, a massive figure moves through the pink trees. It's something I've heard about, but I've never seen before.

It's Jolly.

And he's walking.

Only he's moving naiad-style. This involves roots jutting up from the ground in front of Jolly until they connect to his trunk body. That becomes his right leg. At the same time, the left "leg" recedes into the ground behind him. It's super rare and the sign of an exceedingly old and powerful naiad. His leg branches also glow with the faintest shade of blue. I recognize the color immediately.

It's a shade that's particular to ley lines.

I nibble my lower lip and think this through. Do walking naiads have some ley power in them? It could happen. Jolly's roots have been near ley lines for so long, maybe some of the blue energy just rubbed off over the years.

Jolly slowly lumbers to the top of the hill and settles back in. Within seconds, he looks like the same old Jolly I'd always seen growing up.

I fly over, taking care to hover right in front of Jolly's line of vision, which is about half-way up his trunk. Like always, his features are that of an old man that's droopy, wrinkled, and covered in bark.

I give him a little wave. "Hey, Jolly."

"I'm sleeping and not talking." Jolly's face melts into the bark of the trunk. That means he won't chat anymore, no matter what I do.

I scan Jolly's branches and—*yes!*—my home acorn is still in place. For a second there, I worried that it got knocked off while Jolly was marching around.

There's no point trying to get Jolly to engage, so I shrink myself down and fly inside my home acorn. I find Poppa and Muti snoozing in the dining room. To be exact, they are sleeping with their heads on the tabletop while using their wooden bowls as pillows.

"Hi, guys! I'm home!"

Poppa and Muti slowly sit upright. Like always, they appear as wrinkly little tree sprites with white robes and matching wings. Poppa is also sporting a new sock-cap. It totally works on him.

I hover by the table and wait. It will take Poppa and Muti a while to adjust that I'm here. There's no way I'm missing my hello-hugs.

Sure enough, my parents yawn, smack their lips, and look around the dining room in surprise. Since we live in an acorn, it's a small and curvy space with just a table, chairs, and pictures of me. The moment they realize they have a visitor, their eyes widen.

Muti's the first to go into action. She holds her arms up. "Calla, baby!" I fly over and wrap her in a big hug.

Poppa does the same move. "My turn!"

Once the embraces are done, I settle into my favorite spot at the table. Muti insists on casting me a breakfast of Pixie-O cereal. I eat a few bites before testing out my parents.

"I saw Jolly walking out of the forest," I state.

"Oh, that," says Muti. "He gets wanderlust sometimes."

I jam another bite of Pixie-O's in my face and talk from one side of my mouth. "You never mentioned that he could walk."

Poppa slowly smacks his thin lips. "We always said

Jolly was ancient. Everyone knows senior naiads are mobile."

I chomp down another bite and think this through. My parents are both forty-thousand years old. Jolly's at least that age.

"Did he ever do it when I was a kid?" I ask.

"Sometimes," says Muti. "When you were very little."

"I think I remember that," I say. "The tree would sway like a cradle."

"That's right," says Poppa.

A memory appears. "And whenever we rocked that way, a girl would look down on me from the walls in my room. Remember how I asked you about her?"

"You must have imagined her," explains Muti.

I wince as more of the memory appears. "No, she was in my bedroom with me."

"Not possible," says Poppa. "Besides, that was a long time ago."

Those last words reverberate through me. *A long time ago.* And I get an idea.

Maybe Bilge isn't the only one who knows about the Ogham sword and Usurper. Poppa and Muti may have picked up some lore over the years.

"I've heard a rumor and it isn't pretty," I begin.

"There's nothing you can say that would shock us," says Poppa.

I down my last bite of breakfast before going on. "Word is, the Ogham sword will be found again soon."

Before, my parents were all things cute, sleepy, and old. Now they freak out worse than when I glued myself to Jolly by mistake. (I was five and playing around with fairy dust.)

There's a lot of flying around the dining room and screaming things I can't really understand. Jolly hears and he starts wailing. I can't understand much of what they say, but a few words do stand out. They're pretty terrifying.

Scary Stuff Screamed By Poppa, Muti, and Jolly

"Purge"
"Annihilation"
"New Usurper"
"Argh!"

Clearly, things are not going well.

It takes me a while, but I convince everyone this was just another one of my pranks.

Don't get me wrong. Even after my family calms down, I'm still cranked up inside. My heart pounds so hard, I'm surprised it doesn't break free and take up residence somewhere outside in my body.

But Poppa, Muti, and Jolly are finally chill. I pretend to eat more Pixie-O cereal and play the *remember when game* with my parents. This is more of a spectator sport for yours truly. Here's how it goes.

Remember when you...

...Barfed on Oinky (I was four at the time).

...Ate a pricker flower bush (more barfing followed).

...Shrunk down and danced atop Jolly's nose (this happened a lot when I was three).

...Played pranks on the Elven High Council, the Fartburger Troll Clan, that winter elf who bit Dare, and the mean blue pixie who pushed Oinky in a lake.

Normally, I'd love this conversation. But after listening to Saita? My pranks don't feel as cool anymore. After a while, I try to change the subject.

"What do you think about the fact that I'm queen?"

"It's nice," says Muti.

"We're glad you lived through all your adventures," adds Poppa.

"I've some ideas about things I could fix in the summer realm. There are a lot of injustices."

Poppa and Muti share a long look. I've seen that glance before. It's usually followed by a speech about how I must work harder to fit in. Faeries are mean. I'm too soft-hearted. Blah blah blah.

"I thought that queens just wore nice clothes," says Muti. "Your pink dress looks perfect."

Poppa nods. "And even if some rulers do change things, you don't seem like the type."

I see an opening here and I take it. "Actually, I do have some ideas for improvements."

Poppa shakes his head so hard, his cap falls off. "No, no, n0. Don't make yourself crazy dear."

"Exactly," agrees Muti. "Just do whatever Lazare set up."

"And stay away from the Prince Dare." That's Poppa. "Why?"

"We've heard things," adds Muti.

"Your mother is right. When you said you know some rumors, that's what we thought you'd tell."

"What have you heard about dare? You can tell me anything."

"It's like this," says Muti. "We heard that there's a new plague in Faerie. Dare caused it. He's about to run away onto Earth and avoid justice."

"Hold on, there." I blink hard as I try to process all this. It doesn't happen. "You learned that Dare caused a new plague and is about to run away?"

"Yes," confirms Poppa.

I take it back. I don't need to process anything. I throw up my hands. "That's a lie. Dare would never do that."

"What do we know?" asks Muti. "It's just a rumor."

Poppa blinks a lot, which means he's getting tired. "Perhaps it's time Muti and I went to bed."

I could keep pushing for Dare's innocence, but there really is no point. Rumors are rumors. I said I could handle anything.

"Sure," I reply. "I'll see you the next time I hold court."

"About that," declares Poppa. "Your mother and I are getting old. You don't mind if we skip the rest of your courts, do you?"

I want to scream, *of course, I mind!* You're half of the sentient beings who show up. Without Poppa and Muti, it's just Dare and Bilge in the room.

But I don't say that. After all, I scared Poppa and Muti enough for one day. Maybe that's why they're babbling stuff about Dare being Mister Plague. Plus, my parents are super old. I can't expect they'll spend the day hanging out in my courtroom again. All they do is sleep anyway.

It takes an effort, but I somehow force on a smile. "No problem at all."

I help Poppa and Muti finish their meals and get into

bed. Once they're all settled in, I fly back to the summer palace.

It's tempting to fly over to the Pixieland Citadel and chat up Bilge right now. Two reasons I can't do this. First, Bilge is sleeping. Second, I really must process everything that happened.

I get back to my room and pace around. This is quickly becoming my go-to activity as queen. Hours pass. I come to a major decision. Dare is definitely not a traitor. But Poppa and Muti don't lie, so what does that mean?

Someone wants Dare out of the way. They're planting evil rumors to make it happen… or cover their tracks.

I no sooner come to this decision than the line on my hand turns cold. I accept Dare's visit. Within seconds, the ghostly version of the prince is sitting on my bed.

"You look worried," says Dare.

"I visited Poppa and Muti and heard some news. It seems you're starting a plague and about to sneak off to earth."

"Interesting." Dare taps his chin. "Mother has doubled the guard around the winter palace. She didn't say anything about the Ogham sword or the Usurper, but she must be concerned about this rumor."

"What do you suspect?"

"Someone wants to kidnap me. They set the rumor out so there's a cover." Dare shrugs. "How did it go with Bilge?"

"I hate how you're so calm when using a word like *kidnapping*, especially when it has to do with your own safety."

"It happens all the time," says Dare.

"Not to me."

Dare winces. "Not yet."

My eyes widen. A realization appears. "So when everyone knows that I'll be around for good, then the kidnapping attempts will start?"

"Pretty much."

"At least there's *that* to look forward to." I shake my head. "To answer your other question—Bilge wasn't in the citadel today, but it's clear that he's doing some major brewing. Something big is coming up and it needs potions."

Dare frowns. "Why would the Usurper or Ogham sword need a potion from Bilge?"

I picture all the stuff I've helped Bilge create over the years. "It could be liquid magic enhancer, a draught to foresee the future, an attack brew… there's lots of stuff Bilge might make."

"Whatever is coming, Bilge knows the threat and is

preparing for it. That's what's important. Did you discover anything else from Poppa and Muti?"

"Not from them directly, but…" I shake my head. This still seems unbelievable. "I saw Jolly walk."

Dare's brows lift in surprise. "That's rather troubling. Not sure what it means, but the fact that it's revealed now? I don't trust the coincidence." Dare tilts his head. "How's your back?"

"Still ticklish."

"We better be careful." He float-walks closer, brushes a kiss across my lips, and fades into nothingness.

I make a solemn vow. No matter what, I will find Bilge and get some answers.

Tomorrow.

- Calla

Dear Diary,

This morning, I return to the Pixieland Citadel.

I fly through the main doorway and find Bilge and Oinky waiting in the reception hall. Bilge looks as he always does—a waist-high hobgoblin with a stout body and button eyes. He doesn't even greet me as I fly in.

"You were in my potion master's study yesterday," says Bilge. His voice is ice.

Oinky can sense the tension in the air. He snuffles and speeds out the back door.

Smart Oinky.

"Yes. I saw you brewing up something big."

"Saita has requested some potions. It's a confidential order."

"Is trouble coming?"

"Nothing new. You know how the fire drakes hate the ice dragons. Saita fears they'll start a battle."

"Dare and I visited Errigal. They have both fire drakes and ice dragons. Everyone seemed to be getting along fine."

"That's Errigal." Bilge folds his arms over his chest. "This is a big order for me. I'll have to miss court for the foreseeable future. You don't mind if I stop coming to the summer palace, do you?"

Memories appear. I recall Bilge using stories to make me do things. Somehow, I know this request about the summer palace is along that same line. Trouble is, I don't know what game Bilge is playing and why. But I do know how to answer his question.

"There's a lot of that going around," I say. "I'll be fine."

"You shouldn't be wasting your life in court anyway," declares Bilge. "Take a break. Spend some time playing pranks. That's what makes you great. Everyone has heard of Calla, the amazing prankster."

When Bilge mentioned blowing off court, that didn't bother me. But bringing up the whole prankster thing? That ticks me off.

"I can still be great," I counter. "Only, it will be at something other than pranks. I plan to cast decrees."

Bilge shakes his head. My heart sinks.

That's when I realize what Bilge is really up to. He's trying to get me feeling angry and not thinking clearly. And there are some big intellectual questions here.

I get right to it.

"Why did Poppa and Muti take me in? It seems a really big job for them, considering my birth parents are a king and queen."

"You know the fae. They do strange things."

"Not the Ley Queen and King Tristan. What was so special about Poppa and Muti? Why would my birth parents trust them?"

"I'm sure I don't know." Bilge takes a few steps toward the exit archway. "I should get back to my cauldrons."

"I know Jolly can walk."

"What?" Bilge pauses. "How do you know that?"

"I saw him. Did you know Jolly could do that?"

"Of course. Didn't you?"

"Yes. No. Maybe. I didn't remember until Poppa and Muti explained it. Then I recalled a girl appearing in my room while Jolly marched around. Did I ever say anything to you about that?"

"No." Bilge steps closer. "I guess we can stop the games now. Why are you really here, Calla?"

A question rattles around in the back of my mind.

The moment it comes to the forefront, I know it's the right thing to ask.

"Is the Usurper coming back?"

"Who told you about him?"

"Saita and Lazare." *In a way.*

Bilge sniffs. "Saita and Lazare wouldn't tell you anything. You must have found the secret door in Lazare's chamber of mannequins."

"Secret door?"

"The one that leads to the *real* royal sorcerer's study."

"Right. Sure. That's the one I found."

Bilge steps closer. "May I be honest?"

No conversation ever ended well when it includes *may I be honest*, especially with Bilge. I'm half-tempted to skip the honesty, but Bilge would never say something unless he thought it was important.

"Sure, Bilge."

"You're acting strangely. Unbalanced. Whatever you do, don't cast those decrees. And I'm not the only one who thinks so, either."

Bilge's words feel like more negative nonsense. Still, there's no denying the truth: I have been off my game lately. It's a lot to become queen. Sometimes, I've no idea if I'm doing the right thing. Even worse, so many folks that I trust don't believe I can do this: Ivy, Bilge, Poppa, Muti, Saita… even Ivy's new boyfriend, Vadin.

And in the "Calla can do this" camp, there's only Dare. If I'm being honest, maybe Dare's looking at me in a special way because we just started dating.

"Anything else?" Asks Bilge.

There is, but I'm suddenly feeling way overloaded for now. I step toward the edit. "I've leave you to it, Bilge."

"See you soon, little pixie!"

Bilge said that all the time growing up. Back then, I thought I was a human who soaked in faerie magic, what's called a faeling. Bilge giving me a pet name of *pixie* always felt like an honor.

But now? Something within me breaks.

No one thinks I can do this.

For a hot second, I debate giving up. Then I shrug it off. After all, I've made my decision. Does it sting that so many people don't believe in me? Sure. But that doesn't stop me. I'll still move forward.

After all, Bilge did say one thing that makes me feel awesome. There's another sorcerer's study hidden in my own palace.

I'm finding it tomorrow.

- Calla

*D*ear Diary,

Today, Dare and I return to Lazare's mannequin chamber and look for the hidden door to the real sorcerer's study.

And look.

And look.

We cast spells, knock on walls, and generally make ourselves nuts.

It doesn't help that our original cleaning spell is still at work. Tendrils of magic swirl about, dissolving mannequins and dust bunnies. All the rotten food is already gone from the main room, so things don't smell so gross. But erasing the magical items is the *real* time-suck. Each time the mist hits an enchanted mannequin, the magical vapor soaks into the item until the figure glows pink. Then the spell soaks in and dissolves the thing. Slowly.

It's super distracting.

Frustration tightens across my limbs. It gets so severe, I'm tempted to open a ley door and visit my birth parents. They're powerful magic users—maybe they'll have an idea or two.

I dismiss the idea, though. The Ley Queen and King Tristan have spent ages apart. I don't want to bug them on their second honeymoon unless I'm desperate. As far as I know, the Ogham sword could show up in six weeks or six years. It's not that big of a deal. Yet.

To let off some excess energy, I unfurl my wings and fly around the room. The chamber isn't too big, though. Plus, with all the remaining mannequins and cleaning spells, it's easy to collide with stuff.

Which is what happens.

A major cord of my own power slams into my shoulder, sending me fluttering against the ceiling.

Pop!

I pause. So does Dare.

"Did you hear that?" I ask.

"Yes." Dare unfurls his own wings and hovers beside me. He pounds his fist against the ceiling. "It's hollow."

Anticipation zings through my nervous system. "The door must be up here."

Dare and I keep pounding above our heads until it happens. A section of ceiling magically slides to one side, revealing a dark space beyond.

We fly right in.

The chamber above is a massive space with gray stone walls. In the center of the room, a machine towers thirty feet high. It's made of concentric metal rings.

A sorcerer's wisher.

Dare steps around the huge device. "This can answer any request you make. It's incredibly powerful." He lifts a chunk of metal from the floor. "And broken."

I shake my head. "Lazare must not have known how to use it."

"And yet he tried." Dare runs his hand along one of the massive metal loops. "We used to have one of these at the winter palace. There's a chance this version still has some magic left in it. Perhaps enough for one wish."

"I'm game. How does it work?"

"You're the queen. As far as I know, you say *I wish* and the rest just happens."

I picture my amazing pirate log with me and Dare. Years ago, we wanted answers about the Usurper. Now, we're about to get them.

I take in a deep breath. "I'm Queen Calla, and I wish to know the story of the Ogham sword."

For a moment, nothing happens.

Then great creaks sound as the concentric circles begin to spin. The loops of metal whirl faster. Flooring vibrates. The air hangs with the heavy charge of magic.

A burst of white light fills the room.

Suddenly, we're no longer in the sorcerer's study. Instead, we're walking through an old forest of towering oak trees. This isn't an illusion like a ghost spell. Nope. We're really here. I can scent the pine on the air. Feel the cushy ground beneath my cute ballet slippers. The only sign of magic is how the world's bathed in a distinctly golden light.

An extra-yellow universe. I can live with that.

A handsome elf saunters past me and Dare. A circlet of branches surrounds his head. The man doesn't even know we're near.

Dare grins. "You did it. We've traveled to the past so we can find some answers."

A pair of elves step out from the line of trees. "Coming here to look for your sword again, Usurper?" asks the taller of the two.

"Pathetic null," adds the other.

I take a closer look at the crowned elf. That must be the Usurper. Only he doesn't look anything like the image Dare found all those years ago. This elf is handsome in the classic way of summer elves, from his blond hair to his bright green eyes.

How could someone this perfect turn so foul?

I decide to draw his beauty, just so I never forget what this elf once was.

Usurper

The taller elf stalks up to the Usurper. "Who gave you the right to travel these sacred woods?"

"Queen Emberleigh herself," says the Usurper.

"That's my auntie," quips the tall elf. "I'll mention this to her when I next see her. And if you're lying, you're dead."

The smaller friend smirks. "The queen likes to kill. So it doesn't matter what the truth is. Your life is over."

The elf buddies share a good laugh at this. Which is a total elf thing to do. Don't get me wrong. My father is an elf and a totally great guy. But others of my kind are total creepsters.

The two elves saunter off into the trees. Dare and I watch them leave. A long silence hangs between us as we think through everything we just witnessed.

"Queen Emberleigh," I repeat. "She was alive when Poppa and Muti were young."

Dare nods. "The machine has taken us to a scene from forty-thousand years ago."

Moving deliberately, the Usurper pauses before each oak tree in the clearing. One by one, the elf places his palms against the bark of the trunk and speaks the incantation. Every time, nothing happens.

Dare and I tried this spell when we were kids. Didn't work for us, either.

The Usurper pauses yet another random oak. Only this time, the incantation works.

Root Knight, Root Knight
Holding your magic inside this tree
Root Knight, Root Knight
Open and give your sword to me

Lines of blue light play along the bark, seeping through the intricate wood patterns. The shade of blue is familiar and unique, all at once.

It's a bright shade of sapphire that only happens in ley magic. I see it all the time when I create portals to other worlds.

A memory itches at the back of my mind. I've seen that particular hue recently… and also in an unexpected place. But no matter what I do, I can't quite place the recollection.

The scent of charcoal fills the air. The tree shakes. Branches split and tumble to the ground. The trunk snaps open and recedes. Where once was an oak, there's now a Root Knight holding a massive weapon.

The Ogham sword.

The Root Knight looks just as he did in the drawing I made when I was nine years old. He's a withered old man with bark-covered legs. Branches stretch out from his head and shoulders.

Rustling erupts from the opposite side of the clearing. From the corner of my eye, I catch someone shifting through the shadows between trees. I'm tempted to look away from the Root Knight, but I can't. After so many years, I simply must see what happens next.

With jerky movements, the Root Knight pulls the Ogham sword from the ground. It's a hefty weapon with a wide blade and flat grip—the kind of sword the giant might wield while herding Jack towards the beanstalk. A mighty cry echoes in my mind: *Fe fi fo fum!*

"Be just and wise," says the Root Knight. He hands the great sword to the Usurper. "Cherish all living things."

"Here's my justice." The Usurper jabs the long blade straight through the Root Knight's stomach. A jolt of fear and rage moves through my body.

On reflex, I rush closer. It's an instinct to help the Root Knight and defeat the Usurper. Beside me, Dare does the same. Yet we both stop after a few paces. This is a recreation of events long ago.

There's nothing we can do for the Root Knight now.

The Usurper twists the blade. "I can't take the risk of another Root Knight offering someone else an Ogham sword." He takes in a deep breath and speaks the incantation Bilge told me so long ago.

One for many,
Magic of plenty.
Make me—

Before the Usurper can finish the spell, a six-legged lamb bounds out from the trees and nips the elf on his ankle.

I frown, not believing what I'm seeing. This is a folly lamb, and it's the Faerie version of the human's dodo bird. Our lore says that folly lambs died out because having six legs wasn't so great when it comes to running away from predators.

Looks like that belief might be a little off. Poor folly lambs.

The Usurper roars with anger, yanks the blade from the Root Knight, and jams the weapon into the folly lamb instead.

Why This Is A Super Dicky Move

It's never great to kill any living thing. But this folly lamb is incredibly cute. As in, human merch adorable. The creature is all fluffy pink fur, pointy toes, and big brown eyes. Plus, it gives out a double *baah-baah* sound that just makes you want to rush over and kiss its nose. Who kills something just because it nips your ankle? A super dicky elf, that's who.

Back to the story.

The Usurper then speaks the full incantation.

One for many,
Magic of plenty.
Make me death and bones!

The folly lamb crumples to the ground. Blue light and power shine around the animal's body. All the fur vanishes, along with what's beneath. Within seconds, there's nothing left of the sweet creature except a pile of charred bones.

My heart sinks. The Usurper didn't just destroy this one cute folly lamb. Every one of its kind across all of Faerie just died as well.

A sickly taste crawls into my mouth. The folly lamb didn't vanish to just any shade of blue magic. Again, it's that particular shade of ley power.

Now that sapphire-colored energy creeps across the ground. Threads of blue power move from the lamb's skeleton. All these many lines have one final destination: the Usurper. Magic flows from the ground and into the evil elf's body.

The Usurper changes.

Moments ago, the elf appeared with an ethereal kind of beauty. Now tiny cords of ley magic crawl burn the Usurper's body. Thin tendrils of smoke waft up wherever ley power appears on the Usurper's skin.

I wince. Every creature in Faerie holds some ley magic. Otherwise, fae could never step through one of my portals and visit Earth. But to contain that power in your body? You must be a ley elemental like me or Mother. But the Usurper isn't one of us. Even so, he wants magic so badly, he'll do anything to get it.

This won't end well.

The many lines of ley magic fade from the Usurper's

skin. Wrinkles cover his flesh. For a young elf, the Usurper looks as old as Poppa and Muti.

A chorus of hisses fills the air. I step about in a circle, scanning for any sign of what's causing the noise. Someone was lurking in the forest before. Could they be behind this?

I look to Dare. "What is that?"

Dare shakes his head. "The Usurper just took in the ley power of one folly lamb. Many more died."

My eyes widen as I realize the full scope of what's about to take place. Countless folly lambs just died. All the natural ley power is heading this way.

Someone will need a skin care routine after this is all over.

From every direction, lines of blue power shoot across the ground. The cords glow and twist as they speed toward the Usurper.

Once again, the many lines twist up the elf's body, searing and smoking as they go. The Usurper becomes engulfed in a cocoon of light and power. When the brightness dies down, the Usurper has fully changed. What was once an elf is now a full-fledged sorcerer in a hooded cloak who floats above the ground thanks to all his new magic.

I shiver, remembering the image I once drew of the

Usurper's changed face. What a piece of work. No wonder he keeps his hood drawn low.

The Usurper has another addition to his appearance: six arms. My soul cracks with grief. Those extra appendages are the only remnant of every folly lamb who ever lived.

Matter of fact, the Usurper is a pretty *scary mary* at this point. I'll draw a picture so I can record the awfulness.

Usurper

So this is a pretty yucky situation.

There are now tons of folly lamb skeletons all over Faerie. The Usurper has transformed into a frightening dude who floats around with extra arms. And the Root Knight is still bleeding out on a nearby patch of ground.

This moment is when our old friends, the tall elves, decide to march back into the scene.

"I told you the blue magic ended in here," says the shorter (and doubtlessly soon-to-be-dead) elf.

The taller elf takes in the new and improved Usurper. Then he does what no one ever seems to in these kind of situations. The guy runs for his life.

Good thinking, that.

Sadly, the My Auntie Will Kill You Elf doesn't get two yards before the Usurper chucks his sword right into the taller elf's back. Shortie elf gets away, but somehow I doubt he'll go far.

The Usurper has now skewered an elf with the Ogham sword. Next stop? Say the incantation and wipe out every elf across all of Faerie.

The Usurper floats over to the tall elf and grips the hilt of the Ogham sword. I wince. There's no way I want to see what comes next. Still, I can't look away either.

The Usurper starts to speak in incantation once more.

One for many,
Magic of plenty.
Make me—

But the sorcerer never gets to finish his spell. Somehow, the Root Knight recovered enough to march across the clearing. Before the Usurper can say the words to kill every elf, the Root Knight acts. I've never seen a tree attack anyone before.

That changes now.

The Root Knight slams his branch arm into the back of the Usurper's head. The evil sorcerer falls over, unconscious. The Root Knight then pulls the Ogham sword out of the Usurper's hand and raises the weapon Sword high.

"You deserve to die," declares the Root Knight. "Still, I won't take what wasn't mine to give." The Root Knight jams the blade into the ground. "Those who wield the Ogham sword must cherish all that lives."

The blade flares with blue light. The Ogham sword slowly lowers into the ground. Another thought strikes me.

Ley lines return home.

At the same moment, the Usurper's unconscious form also descends into the earth. When he wakes up, someone won't be a happy boy.

"It is over for me," whispers the Root Knight. "My second shall take my place. I am thankful to have friends that helped me live this long."

An object falls out of the Root Knight's hand. It's something shiny and clear, but I'm too far away to make out the item clearly. Plus, there are much bigger things going on.

Like the Root Knight dying.

The trees around the clearing rumble and creak. It's as if they know what's about to happen, same as I do. The Root Knight slumps. His body crumbles. Where once stood a mighty warrior, there is now only a pile of dust.

In the hubbub, I forget about the Usurper. But the guy is awake now and fighting against being sucked underground. Fortunately, it's a losing battle.

"I have enough magic now!" cries the Usurper. "I shall come back when the sword returns!"

With that, the Usurper finally gets yanked underground and shuts his stupid yap.

I march over to check out what the Root Knight dropped. It's a potion vial marked with unique runes.

"What is it?" asks Dare.

"Bilge brewed this. It's one of his finest healing portions. He must have known the Usurper would attack the Root Knight, so he gave the guy something to help him live."

Dare nods. "It's just like Bilge said in his story all those years ago. Good fae got together and stopped the Usurper."

A panel of blue light appears nearby. This is something else I've seen before, many times. A ley portal. The brightness congeals into the shape of a heavy iron door.

My pulse speeds. No one but me and Mother can easily cast ley portals on the fly. Will I see the Ley Queen in the past?

The portal swings open.

Saita and Bilge step into the clearing. Both look surprisingly similar to how they do today. How old are these two, anyway?

In her right hand, Saita holds a magic wand that flares with blue light. No question about it. That thing is loaded with ley power. I nod once. That explains how they were able to transport here. Ley wands are extremely rare and expensive, but they do exist.

"We shouldn't linger," says Bilge.

"I know," states Saita. "We saw what happened in my magic mirror, but I must see it with my own eyes as well." She scans the clearing before kneeling at the spot where the Root Knight fell. Saita sets her palm against the ground. "The Root Knight is truly gone." She rises and steps over to the place where the Usurper lowered into the ground. "But the Usurper will come back."

"Are you satisfied?" asks Bilge. "No one can know what happened here."

"Yes, I am. We'll must find that other elf and erase his memories."

"I can brew something for that."

Poor Bilge. He really hates leaving the citadel for any reason, let alone to visit a crime scene.

"We must find the next Root Knight," declares Saita.

"And discover when the Ogham sword will appear once more."

Bilge scans the trees nervously. "I can uncover that information."

Saita raises her right brow only. It's a very queenly expression which I must master in my spare time. "How will you manage that? Another potion?"

Bilge's sideways ears tremble. That means he's getting angry. "I'm not the only magic user in the Pixieland Citadel, you know. Most of the greatest witches and wizards study within our walls. We'll figure it out."

For a moment, I try to picture the Pixieland Citadel as overflowing with magic users of all kinds.

Nope. Can't do it.

For as long as I've known him, Bilge has always been a solo guy. And all the other citadels are deserted, so it's not like he can swap magic tips across Faerie. This news explains a lot actually. Mostly, I can see why Bilge got so attached to me. As a rule, hobgoblins don't hang with anyone outside their familiars. Bilge must have lost many friends.

White light floods the clearing. Mechanical whirs fill the air. The noise soon turns so loud, I'm forced to cover my ears. Swooping lines appear in the recesses of the forest. It's the machine from back in my palace, doing its thing to end the spell.

The sorcerer's wisher.

The light burns more brightly than ever before. Chunks of metal go flying through the air. Dare presses me against the ground, covering my body with his. Bits of metal go flying. Snaps sound as the machine breaks apart.

The illusion of the forest vanishes. Dare and I are back in the secret sorcerer's study. What was once a massive machine is now a pile of smoking junk. Another burst of white light erupts from the center of the room and even that burned-out hulk vanishes. The entire place is empty.

That's not what really grabs my attention, though. The main event right now is how Dare's body fits so perfectly atop mine.

The prince gives me a sly look. "We can't do this now, Calla."

"Boo."

Dare hops to his feet and offers me his hand. "Are you alright?"

I slip my palm against his. It isn't as nice as full-body contact, but at this point, I'll take what I can get. "I'm fine. You?"

"I got a few hits, but nothing my body armor couldn't handle."

"And all this time, I thought you were just being paranoid, wearing that stuff constantly."

Dare winks. "You'd be surprised."

With the excitement of *Dare time* being over, my thoughts round back to everything we saw in the sorcerer's wisher. It's a ton to process, so I start with the basics.

"No wonder Saita doesn't want me doing anything," I begin. "That Usurper guy is a freak."

"True enough. After what we just saw, I believe Mother is handling the stress rather well."

I hug my elbows. "I won't say the same for Bilge. I can't believe he'd lie to us about the…" I want to finish my sentence, but the words won't come.

Dare finishes my thought. "Ogham sword."

"Bilge is my mentor and friend. Not that I put him on this super-high pedestal. It's more of a medium-tall one."

"I'm sure he's doing what he thinks will protect us both. Last time, his plan and potions stopped the Usurper. I bet Bilge and Saita think that'll work again."

I rub my neck and try to think this through. "Remember how you found that picture of the Usurper in your library? I bet it was in a book Saita borrowed from Bilge."

Dare nods. "Half our library does come from the Pixieland Citadel." He frowns. "There's one thing I don't understand. How would a potions master even know about the Usurper to begin with?"

"We must talk to Bilge directly."

"What about your parents? Bilge is very close to them. Maybe they know something, too."

"The other day, I just mentioned the Ogham sword to them. Poppa and Muti got really upset. I couldn't even get anything logical out of them. Let's see what Bilge can share first."

"Makes sense." Dare gestures around the room. "In the meantime, you now have a superb spot for your witchy workroom. This place is laden with remnant energy." He steps closer. "You may even have a prince willing to help your casting." He tilts his head. "Unless you want to wait?"

I smile my face off. "No way. Let's do this."

"Have you set your plans?" asks Dare.

"You know it." When you create a building or what-ever, you must have a specific design in mind. Other-wise, the magic does what it wants. That's always a disaster.

"Fire up your casting," says Dare. "I'll add in extra energy."

I'm so excited, I don't even whistle for Sammy to show up and add more magic. Normally, my scepter is my back-up when extra energy is required. But with Dare around?

Power ho.

Closing my eyes, I pull on the magic that constantly whirls inside me. Pink fairy dust materializes above my palms. I order the energy to create my perfect workroom. Tendrils of glowing magic coil off from my hands. The many cords of power twist and dive around the chamber.

Dare summons his own wintry energy. Small tornadoes of glowing snow spin about the floor.

As our magic goes to work, I picture everything I want in my witchy workroom. There will be cauldrons. Potion ingredients. Long-forgotten books. A broom (this doesn't really do anything but it looks cool). And I add in a little play area for Sammy, as well as something for myself. While Sammy will get his playpen, I'll have a door that leads to my very own bouncy castle.

What perfection.

It's late by the time we finish casting. Dare and I decide to visit Bilge tomorrow together. Now that we know what's about to happen, one big question remains.

When?

It's the type of conversation that works best when Dare and I tag-team Bilge. With that decision made, the prince flies off to his home castle and I crawl into bed. I'm asleep before I pull the covers under my chin. It's a good thing, too. I need the rest.

Another big day lies before me.

- Calla

Dear Diary,

Dare and I meet up at the Pixieland Citadel first thing in the morning. *Ish.*

Normally, I just shrink myself down—using pixie dust, naturally—and fly in through a window. But with Dare along, that's not really an option. So we knock on the front door and wait.

After what feels like forever, Bilge finally opens the door. This morning, my hobgoblin buddy is all droopy ears and a puffed-out lower lip. I've seen this expression before. Bilge is an unhappy guy.

Oinky snuffles happily around Bilge's feet. He really is a cute pig. Bilge motions between his familiar and the opened door. "Why don't you go outside and play?"

Oinky makes a sound that I call his *yipe-snort*. Then he hides behind Bilge's ankle.

Crouching down, Bilge pats Oinky's head. "It's nothing bad, little friend."

I bite my lips together, hard. *Nothing bad? This is about the end of all life in Faerie.*

"Fine," says Bilge. "It is a little worrisome. Still, I must speak with Dare and Calla alone."

That does the trick. Oinky slowly prances out the door. If pigs can give their hobgoblin buddies the side-eye, then that's what Oinky does now.

"Come on in," says Bilge. "Close the door behind you."

Dare and I share a long look. "He knows," I say.

"And he's ready," confirms Dare.

For those who don't speak Calla-Dare, that exchange means that Bilge already realizes we're here about the Usurper. The hobgoblin is ready to spill his guts. Figuratively.

Bilge marches off to the old library. This is a big deal. All the books Bilge likes are in his private collection upstairs. The old library is a massive room with curved walls, tons of books, and even more cobwebs.

For the first time, I consider why Bilge never goes in here. In the trip through time, Bilge talked about having other magic users in the Citadel. Maybe they kept all their stuff in this library.

A pang of sympathy moves through me. Whatever's about to happen, I appreciate Bilge opening some old wounds to help out.

As a hobgoblin, Bilge isn't exactly super tall or athletic. I wouldn't have him any other way. Dare and I follow Bilge as he toddle-walks into the library and pauses before the main hearth. There's no fire in it, per usual.

"You want to talk about the Usurper, no doubt." Bilge doesn't wait for an answer. Instead, he pulls a small vial from his pocket. "I expected this." Bilge tosses the small container of potion into the fireplace. The glass container smashes and releases a puff of violet smoke. An electric charge of magic fills the air. Purple mist spreads throughout the air.

The haze congeals into a vision that overlays onto the library itself. It's a lot like when I visit Dare as Ghost Calla. The library is still there, only there's a new and semi-transparent reality on top of things.

And what that magic vision reveals is nothing less than amazing.

The magical library is crammed with magic users. There are men, women, pixies, nixies, banshee, Sidhe...

you name it. People are almost crawling over each other as they vie for the best books.

One figure stands out from the rest. It's the Usurper. The guy is back to his handsome self. And he's talking to a past version of Bilge.

"You know the Usurper was a magical null," says current-day Bilge. "What you don't know is that he was my student."

"I didn't know you were a teacher," I state. "Beyond me, I mean."

Current Bilge shoots me a sad smile. "I taught potions here for more than two thousand years. It was one of the few areas of study where you didn't need any magical ability to create low-level spells. I took in the Usurper because, well…" Current Bilge turns and gestures toward the misty versions of himself and the Usurper.

For the first time, I notice what everyone else in the room is really doing. They're only *pretending* to fight over books. In reality, they're aiming dirty looks at the Usurper. A pair of sprites giggle behind their hands. A handsome summer elf—the very My Auntie Will Kill You Guy from the future—glares hot death at the back of the Usurper's head.

"Let me guess," says Dare. "The Usurper was the only null studying at the citadel."

"That's right," replies Current Bilge. "The other students thought he didn't deserve to be here. Or that I only took him in because his parents were mean enough to name him the Usurper."

I raise my hand. "It would have been a factor if I ran the place."

"And it was in my case, believe me." Current Bilge gestures to the top of a towering wall. I'd never noticed it before, but there's a line of windows up there. And beyond the dirty glass, I can make out another hobgoblin. This guy is a little wider than Bilge and has three eyes.

"Who's that?" I ask.

"That's the Inverness. He's a sorcerer and motions master who used to run the Pixieland Citadel. And he taught me everything I know. It was the Inverness who informed me about the Ogham sword. I wanted to make the Usurper feel special, so I shared the tale with him as well." Current Bilge shakes his head. "What a disaster. The boy became obsessed with the idea of using the Ogham to gain true magical ability."

Current Bilge waves his arm. The magical vision dissipates. Within seconds, we're back in the regular old library again. "It was the Usurper who figured out when the Ogham sword would next appear. I'm guessing that's why you came here today. You want to know if we face an imminent threat."

In this moment, I'd love to scream something like, *what the hell, Bilge? I'm Queen of the Summer Fae! Of course, I must know when a homicidal-n-magical nut job will show up and start turning my subjects into skeletons.* But I'm able to control myself like an incredibly regal and mature person.

"It would be helpful," I state.

"The Root Knight is powered by the connection between Earth and Faerie. Ley magic. When that link between worlds becomes too strong, the override of power releases the Root Knight and Ogham sword."

I take a half step backward. Years of Bilge's lectures spin through my mind. A realization hits me. "Once every forty thousand years, an equinox will reach its peak at the very same moment, both on Earth and in Faerie. That's what does it, isn't it?"

Bilge nods. "Yes. The Root Knight and Ogham sword will always appear at the harmonic equinox."

For a long moment, Dare stares around the room while making silent calculations. "Faerie time is more fluid than its human counterpart. If I'm not mistaken, then the harmonic equinox could happen any time between the next two days and two months."

"That's correct," states Bilge. "We'll know because the

sun will change colors. The last harmonic Equinox had a yellow hue. This time, the world will be bathed in red. The color will grow more intense as the moment of equinox's height approaches... and as you get closer to the Root Knight's oak tree."

"Great," I state. "When Dare and I combine forces, we can wield some serious magic. Once the world goes red, we'll head right over to the Root Knight, grab the Ogham sword, and stop the Usurper before he starts."

"No," says Bilge gently. "I've lost so much, Calla. I can't lose you. And Saita feels the same way about Dare. Last time, the winter queen and I stopped the Usurper together. We did it before; we'll do so again."

Dare narrows his eyes. "And what do you plan, exactly?"

"It will be the same as last time: Distract the Usurper and steal the sword from him."

Which is a crap plan.

"What about Poppa and Muti?" I ask. "Do they have a role in all this?"

A guilty look might cross Bilge's face, but it's gone too quickly to be certain.

"Your parents know enough to be frightened," says Bilge. "That is all. I hope you won't scare them again, Calla."

That's what you call a non-denial denial. And it deserves a non-confirming confirmation.

"I'd never hurt Poppa and Muti if I could avoid it," I declare.

Bilge seems to accept this. "Thank you. I hope you both keep this between us. Poppa and Muti aren't the only ones who are easily upset. Saita is almost frantic. You must step out of this situation, Dare."

"I can't promise that," says Dare. "I understand this plan worked for you before, but that's all the more reason to avoid it a second time. The Usurper has been waiting thousands of years for another chance at the Ogham sword. My bet is that he's spent most of that time replaying the day he got pulled into the ground... and planning how he'd do it better next time."

Bilge lifts his chin. "All I ask is for you to wait. Give the plan from me and Saita a chance to work. If we fail, then you two you can do whatever you wish."

Dare and I share a long look. Then we exchange the smallest of nods.

"We'll try to let you do your thing," I state. "But the minute things go sideways, we'll step in."

"But you have to let Calla announce her decrees," adds Dare.

Which is a good idea.

Bilge shoots me a sad smile. "If you insist."

"We do," I state.

Bilge purses his lips for a moment. "Fine. See you at the Harmonic equinox."

With that, Dare and I leave. Now that we know our timeline, we've got some planning to do.

\- Calla

DAY 104

$\mathcal{D}$ear Diary,

Today Dare and I work on our plan to defeat the Usurper. Sure, we promised Bilge to let him try his scheme first. But let's face it—that's going to suck. We must have something ready that works.

To begin with, we decide this is all about defending the sword versus kicking butt (although that will probably happen, too). Castles use concentric defense walls. If one barrier goes down, you haul ass to the next one. That's our idea here.

Dare And Calla's Master Plan

First wall: reach the Ogham Tree. Whatever it takes, we must get there before anyone else. That'll put a hitch in the Usurper's giddy-up. But if that doesn't work…

Second wall: protect the sword. Let's say the Usurper beats us to the tree. Dare and I will stab the evil sorcerer with pokey things and attack magic. Anything to keep him away from the Ogham. This leads to a big discussion about whether to bring along an army or not. We decide to go with a small strike force. Big armies and heavy forests do not mix.

Third wall: retake the sword. This one is hard to think about. If the Usurper somehow gets the Ogham, then Bilge plans to distract the Usurper and grab the sword. The Usurper knows this tactic is coming and will be prepared.

Long story short, we think our best bet is to stop the Usurper long before he gets anywhere near the Ogham. Once a mega-evil sorcerer has the magical tool in hand to destroy the world, your options really get limited.

And that's our plan.

Posterity, you're welcome.

- Calla

*D*ear Diary,

Today, I plan to hang in my witchy workroom and check how things are progressing. And in all honesty? I really want to play in my bouncy castle. Hey, if you had one nearby, then you'd be thinking the same thing, believe me.

I'm about to head when Sammy boings into my bedroom. Once he's close, Sammy changes from his regular round form into a donut shape.

And then he sits on my head, crown style.

"Let me guess," I state. "I must visit my court chamber?"

Sammy slides off my noggin to bounce around the room.

That's a big *yes*.

There's no royal court scheduled for today, so I assume there are more nonsense questions for me. It's probably the same deal as with the guards. If my subjects don't see me, then they figure out their whole day without asking me a million dumb things. But if I'm near? It's like their brains shut down or something. And this is very different from being taken seriously on major subjects that have to do with running the realm, mind you.

In any case, it all circles down to one fact: whatever this is, it's probably nothing.

That's why I wear in my regular minidress as I step through the neon yellow hallways that lead to the court chamber. When I reach the outer doors, I find Ivy leaning against a nearby stretch of wall.

She's alone.

"Hey, Ivy!" I race up and pull her into a big hug. The embrace is not returned. It's like wrapping my arms around a plank of wood. "Where's Vadin?"

At last, Ivy meets my gaze. Her eyes are lined with tears. "I don't want to talk about him!"

When I next speak, I take care to use my most soothing tone. "Okay, that's fine. We don't have to discuss Vadin."

For the next twenty minutes, Ivy proceeds to monologue about—you guessed it—Vadin.

It all starts with how Ivy and this other girl, Holly, have hated each other since forever. Now Holly's great-great-somebody has died and left her the title of Lady Holly. Which makes *nemesis chickie* a noble while Ivy stays a nobody. And now Holly's making moves on Vadin. Which wouldn't be a problem except Vadin's family wants a noble marriage and he hasn't been at the unicorn stables for hours and hours. It's terrible.

I wait until Ivy's been silent for a full five seconds before responding. "I think Vadin is really into you."

"Are you sure?"

The true answer is this: *I have no idea.* Dare and I have dated for less than two weeks. How can I be an expert on relationships? But the big goal here is to help Ivy feel better, so I reach right into my little bag of white lies.

"I'm positive. You two are happening." An idea appears. Once the thought occurs to me, I can't believe I didn't think of it right away. "I know how to fix this."

I let out a low whistle. Sammy boings down the hall to land in my hand in his awesome scepter form. I tap Ivy's shoulders with his golden coolness.

"What's that about?"

"Holly is a Lady? Well, I just made you a Super Lady. And I'll give you some palace land, too. You like the lake?"

"Of course. Everyone loves the Mermaid Retreat. But are you sure you can part with it?"

"It's mine, right? I never even go there. Now, it's yours. Bippity boppity boo. All done. So stop your worrying. I'm sure Vadin is off scooping up unicorn poop somewhere. He'll be back any second now."

After I finish this speech, a curl of golden sparkles rises from the end of my scepter. The bits land on Ivy's head, where they take the shape of loopy circlet. If you check out this mini-crown closely, the whirls make out some words: *Mermaid Retreat.*

So that's how I give out titles and lands. Now I know.

Ivy pats her temple with her fingertips. "I have a circlet now? Wow! I'm a real lady."

"A real Super Lady," I correct.

Ivy wraps me in a hug. Unlike the last embrace, this one is totally genuine. "Thank you, Calla." Ivy starts to run off and pauses. "Oh, we never talked about your sleigh ride with Dare."

"Eh, that has to wait a while. All of Faerie could end any time within the next two days or two months. I'm pretty booked up."

Ivy's mouth falls open. Long seconds tick by. Then my friend laughs so hard, tears stream down her cheeks. "Another prank! You really got me that time!" Ivy races off toward the stables.

And I come to a major realization.

I've been looking at this *you're a prankster thing* all wrong. Once people figure out that I mean business, they'll hang on my every word. I'll have to keep a directory for all the half-truths I'll need to use.

But for now? Not a problem. I can blab anything. Folks won't believe me because of the prankster thing.

I'm feeling pretty amazing about my newfound perspective as I step up to the main doors to my court chamber. My two guards stand outside. Both crook their fingers at me. These are the guys I used to call Blond and Blonder. Their real names are Sargent Pickle and Private Elderberry. Since they're some of the few folks who talk to me without tasking me out on minor crap, I must remember their real names.

I step up to Blond and Blonder. "What is it, Sargent Pickle and Private Elderberry?" Hopefully, it's not too obvious I'm working their names into every interaction. Breaking the *Blond and Blonder habit* isn't easy.

"You have an actual elf subject in your courtroom," says *guy who I'm pretty sure is Sargent Pickle.*

"Really? I do?"

"Yes." It's Private Elderberry this time (probably). "That's why we sent Sammy to find you. Will you play a prank on them?"

I bob my head, considering. "Eh, it depends who they

are." I knock on the closed doors. "Let me in and I'll take a look."

The guards whip open the main door and I stroll into my court chamber. I haven't redecorated this spot yet, so the place is still Lazare decor, meaning it has the golden walls, floor, and everything else. The metal throne is the only thing I've updated. It's now a chair made of roses. Not always super comfortable, but it looks gorgeous.

I'm not halfway across the floor when I almost face-plant into an elf lady.

And not just any elf—this is a noble named Lady Kae. She's been high on my *hit list of folks to meet*. Mostly because she's got the most changelings of anyone in my realm. I'll add in a picture of how she looks since it's important to our upcoming conversation.

Oh, and I also hate her guts.

Lady
Kae

id I mention I hate Lady Kae? I do.

When we last left my life, I'd just face-planted into Lady Kae. After that, she gracefully steps aside in a move that says, *you may now pass, oh queen of clumsiness.*

I don't take a step.

Instead, I stay in place and stare at Lady Kae for a very long time. This is what the Elven High Court used to do when they brought me in to complain about my pranks and stuff. It didn't work on me, but it's worth a try here.

It's not that *whoever talks first loses*, but Lady Kae does start off the conversation.

Loser.

"I'm here because I heard rumors," declares Lady Kae.

"Do you always start conversations this way with royalty?"

"Oh, pardon me." Lady Kae looks like she'd rather eat dirt than speak her next words. "Greetings, your Majesty."

"There's a bow you should add in, but we can work on that later. What seems to be the problem?"

"I have my contacts among the palace staff. What they're saying is outrageous."

All of a sudden, I realize that I've made a few strategic errors here. Namely, I'm not on my throne and wearing my combo gown-n-crown. I could high tail it over there now, but then it would look like Lady Kae is intimidating me.

Which she isn't.

Mostly.

"Let's hear it," I say. Then I clear my throat and go for a second round. "Or rather, tell me what thou heardest."

Heardest? Is that a word? Who knows. Hopefully, it sounds more regal.

"The man you share courtship rings with is planning to release a plague."

"His name is Prince dare and I've heard that lie already." I shrug. "Not worried. Anything else?"

"The council believes the only way to stop Dare is for you to kill him."

"Wow. Someone needs to cut back on their catnip. I am not killing anybody. If this rumor keeps going, then I'll just clear Dare's name. Problem solved."

"But you must see the risk. If anything should happen to Dare, everyone will blame you."

"The subject of Prince Dare is off-limits."

Why, oh why, did I want to talk to nobles? This is worse than palace staff asking me which way to unroll the toilet paper.

"Nice to meet you," I say quickly. "I've got lots to do, so we can catch up another time." I start to walk away when Lady Kae speaks again.

"It's also rumored that you want to choke the life out of nulls like me."

I stop in my tracks. Inch by inch, I turn around. "You mean…" I mime choking.

"Not literally, my queen. I was blessed with great beauty, long life, and a sharp mind. Yet I wasn't given your natural gifts for magic."

"And?"

I know where she's going with this, but I want to hear her say it.

"I'm a null. That's why I need my changelings forever."

"Hm, let me consider that." I tap my cheek. "No."

"You cannot pass this decree. It won't work. I'm not sure where you got the idea to even try. Why don't you just do more pranks?"

"Well, I *am* ending the Elven High Council. Does that count as a prank?"

"You're doing what to *my* High Council?" She gasps. "I hadn't heard that."

"Well, now you know. Instead, I'm creating a new *Everyone Council.* I'll make sure some nulls are on it as well. The solution to you having limited skills isn't to treat other people like garbage."

"You have no right to do such a thing."

I give Sammy a little shake. "My scepter and I disagree."

"It must be obvious. All of Lazare's children have refused to even consider the throne."

"Lotti wanted it."

"You exploded her."

"She sort-of exploded her self but *yes.* That was a real shame and everyone feels super bad about it. And your point is?

"I'm Lazare's illegitimate daughter."

"Okay. That explains a lot."

Lady Kae taps the center of her chest. "I'm next in line for the throne. If anything happens to you, I become queen. You can't make decisions that change my realm without my knowledge. You need my guidance."

"I disagree," I state. "I've gotten magical reports on your lands. If I need help making humans dance themselves to death at the revels, then you'll be my go-to chick. But other than that? Nothing. "

"Revels are an elvish tradition."

"So dance on your own. Don't make humans do it for you."

"You don't understand. I attended the Elfish Academy for comportment. I look the part of a queen. I've lived my entire life in court. I *deserve* this."

"Oh, I get it." *Which is true.* "You've put yourself together today in order to highlight everything you *think* I'm not, from your comportment talk to your fancy dress. You're trying to show how you'd be a better queen. Everything you do is calculated to intimidate me. It won't work."

"We'll see." Lady Kae marches toward the exit. Fortunately for me, my courtroom is a rather big place, so she has a long way to go. While her back is turned in my direction, I point Sammy toward the floor and picture my spell.

Or rather, my prank.

Sammy understands me perfectly. An orb of golden power hovers before me. Closing my eyes, I give a few final instructions to my spell. When I reopen my eyes, the sphere is gone. My trap is set.

Now it's just time to see if Lady Kae will walk into it.

In classic Grinchy style, I cup my hand by my ear and listen. Sure enough, there's the telltale clink of someone lifting a *metal something* from the floor. And silence as this person steps away.

Which means Lady Kae just picked up what she thinks is my crown from from the floor. Really, anyone this greedy and stupid deserves what they get.

And get it, Lady Kae does.

A shrill voice echoes into the court chamber. "Work it, supermodel!"

That would be lady Kae, who is now trapped in a dancing spell for the next three days. If she'd just handed over my fake crown instead of trying to steal it, then my revels spell wouldn't have kicked in.

But she is a thief. And now she's a dancer. Good times.

With Lady Kae taken care of, I'm ready to head back to my regularly-planned day of bouncy castle happiness. The guards swing open the doors once more.

"Dame Guinevere to see you," says Sargent Pickle or Private Elderberry.

I frown. "Who?"

"She's from the Errigal."

"Oh. She must have been one of the folks who saw me the other day with the fire drake vizier. Show her in."

And so, Dame Guinevere steps into the chamber. She's a lovely summer fae in the spirit of Ivy. Only, while Ivy has some sprigs of green on her dress, Dame Guinevere wears a full garden of flowers in her hair.

Dang, does she ever look familiar, too. Sadly, I can't place her. Maybe drawing Dame Guinevere will help me recall where I've seen her before.

Dame Guinevere

Nope. Drawing Dame Guinevere doesn't help.

We speed through the formal greetings stuff. Since Dame Guinevere is with the Errigal, she's not technically my subject. We can skip to the good stuff.

"What's up?" I ask.

Guinevere blushes. "I just wanted to meet you face to face. The way you pull those ley lines in Errigal… it's so impressive."

"Let's just say I didn't have a lot of adult supervision as a child. I developed certain skills. Nothing to do with desert living, though."

Guinevere frowns. "What do you mean?"

"When you saw me in Errigal."

"Still don't follow."

This is way strange. The only time I've ever been to Errigal is when we visited the talking Desert. Still, maybe Guinevere is trying to keep their latest location a secret.

"Never mind," I say.

"Okay." Dame Guinevere smiles. "Now that you're close, I can see how you glimmer with ley magic."

No one's ever said that to me before. I decide to take it as a compliment.

"You're a fine ruler to your people," adds Guinevere. "I couldn't help but overhear what Lady Kae said. What if you die? What will happen to the summer fae?"

"Oh, I won't put Lady Kae in charge, if that's what you're worrying. I'll cast a spell so Bilge must find my successor."

"And if he's gone?"

"Then Dare and Saita can decide. They'd make a good pick. Why are you so concerned, anyway?"

"Things are better now that you're queen, even in Errigal. Protector Lazare used to send assassins after us. We don't want that to change if anything happens to you."

"Don't worry. I'll be fine."

"But everyone says you can only do pranks. Soon you'll fail, get cast off the throne, or worse."

Wow. Guinevere lives on the backside of nowhere and even she knows about my prank situation.

Time for yet another tactical retreat.

"So, there's nothing you want from me?"

"Just to meet you."

"Well, it's been nice chatting, but I must check on my witchy workroom. Also, I've hit my daily quota of people telling me I'm only good for pranks."

Guinevere looks confused. "Thank you."

My guards do a good job of ushering her out the door. With that weirdness behind me, I finally make my way to my witchy workroom. The spells are still working away, with little tendrils building out vials, books, and whatnot.

Still no bouncy castle yet. Bummer.

All of a sudden, my hand turns icy cold. It's another ghost-call from Dare. I don't even need to check on what the chat is about… or consider whether to participate. Without the bouncy castle, I've got time to kill.

I whisper to my palm. "I accept your visit."

Ghost Dare appears. "I have good news. Mother has agreed to discuss the Usurper with me. Want to join the chat?"

"It depends. Does she know I'll be there?"

"Absolutely not."

"Okay, just be sure to keep the smelling salts handy. When are you thinking?"

"How about tomorrow? We're having ice polo games. Care to watch?"

It takes everything in me not to screech like a fool while jumping up and down. But I stay totally calm and queen-like.

Here's the deal with ice polo. These games happen in what counts for summertime in Dare's realm. That means there's a shifting four-hour window when there isn't an insane amount of ice on a place called Tundra Lake. The players can actually get into the chilly water and do their thing. And as for the game itself? Dare rides frost ponies while wearing nothing but shorts. Boom.

I've wanted to see these games my entire life. Yet every time that magical window opens, I always have a test to take with Bilge or a birthday party with Poppa and Muti. But now? The world is mine. Or at least, I've got some ice pony polo coming.

I do my best to sound casual. "I guess I can make it."

"See you tomorrow, then?"

"I'll be there." With bells on. Or maybe my own swimsuit. A girl needs to take opportunities where she can find them.

That night, I fall right asleep. Maybe it's the thought

of Lady Kae dancing around her changelings that puts
me at ease.

There really is nothing better than a good prank.

- Calla

DAY 106

*D*ear Diary,

    It's ice pony polo day!

This is a lifelong goal for yours truly, so it must be handled carefully. And by that, I'm talking about one key concept here…

Reconnaissance.

All of which is why I first visit the games as Ghost Calla. This way, I can scope put the grounds without causing undue attention.

Or in the case of Saita, an early heart attack.

Tundra Lake is a wide expanse of open ice under a gray sky. Tiny whirls of snow dance across the frozen liquid. For the purposes of the games, a great oval of arched ice marks the periphery of the tournament space. Picture an oblong glass donut, cut the thing in half longwise, and then drop the clear demi-loop on a frozen lake. That's pretty much the set-up for ice pony polo.

On one short end of the oval, there are a series of blocky buildings for players and whatnot. Since these are winter elves, everything is made from ice, not glass. And also, nothing is heated. The "buildings" are meant to keep wind and snow out of your eyes. If this place is too cold for you, then the locals figure you probably aren't an ice elf anyway. Best to go home.

There are also a pair of tall judge's chairs on either "skinny side" of the oval. In one seat, there's an actual elf judge. He's got blue skin (it's natural, not from the cold), pointy ears, and long silk shorts. A silver whistle hangs around his neck. The guy is acting like the cold doesn't bother him at all, but I can see the tell-tale sign of a warming spell glowing just above his flesh. Everyone's wearing them today. And they all pretend they aren't.

Winter elves. Go figure.

Now we come to the *me part of the day*. The second judge's chair appears to be empty. But that's a lie. I'm parked there while in Ghost Calla mode. The audience can't see me at all, and I stay warm as a sunbeam.

This is so fun.

The elf judge blasts his whistle. Over inside the viewing donut, the winter elves jockey for a good spot by the glass-like ice wall overlooking the playing space.

Folks wear different styles of leathers and furs, all in shades of blue, black, or white. Latecomers spread their wings and hover above the standing crowd. It takes up more energy to fly through a whole game, but at least you don't have anyone's elbow in your rib cage.

There's one section midway across the donut that's pretty empty. No crowds. Only a few fancy chairs fill the space.

Huh.

That's got to be the equivalent of elfy box seats. Sure enough, I can make out Saita sitting in there. It won't be easy for her to escape that spot and complain. You know, just in case something might happen.

You never know.

Once again, the judge blasts his whistle. The lake shimmies. My tall viewing chair wobbles from side to side. Long cracks form along the playing ground.

Smash! Twelve ponies break through the ice. All have blue fur and matching bat-style wings. A single rider sits atop each steed while gripping a polo mallet.

More crashes sound as a pair of goalposts rise up from the ice. There's one for each short-end of the playing area.

The judge lets out a final blast from his whistle. A small blue orb rises up from the ice. The ice pony polo ball. From here, things get crazy. I'm not sure who's on what team. The ball gets whacked from one player to another with such speed, it's hard to keep track.

At first, anyway.

After a while, I start to follow the rhythm of play. And I definitely enjoy watching a shirtless Dare swing his polo mallet around.

The thought hits me. After so many years of waiting for my chance to catch a match, who knows when I'll have another opportunity like this one? And what's the point of being a master of ley magic if I can't use it to zip home *quick like a bunny*, change into a bikini, cast a few warming spells, and then crash this match?

The more I contemplate this idea, the better I like it. In short order, I've unghosted myself from the game, gone home, and gotten ready. My selected bikini for the occasion is pink and my chosen warming spells come from Sammy. This gives my skin a golden glow.

Take that, winter elves.

Next, I pull up some ley lines and open a door directly from my bedroom to the women's changing house behind the main playing area.

I pull the door open and step through. Unlike the viewing donut, everything in here is dark as concrete. Which makes sense, considering now folks need privacy and all that. A little cold nips my skin, but nothing too bad. I scope out the scene. The building is your basic rectangle. It's a one story high space with walls that are lined with tall cubbies (all made from ice). Long benches divide up the floor.

No one's around, though.

Which is odd.

I planned my visit so I'd arrive at half-time. Plenty of female players are in today's game. This place should be filled with blue-skinned girls chatting up the best ways to hold a mallet or whatever.

Someone clears their throat. I turn around and there he is.

Dare.

And the prince is standing in such a way to block the only entrance or exit from the space.

"Hello, Calla."

"Hey."

I do my best to look casual in a bikini. It isn't easy. I had a much different plan for this situation. In a matter of minutes, one player would encounter an untimely—but ultimately harmless—accident. A new player would enter the game, kick ass, and make history.

That would be me.

"I thought this might happen," says Dare. "And when your ghost self disappeared, I knew it was true."

"Where are all the girl players?"

"I used my royal influence to move them to a different prep space for half-time."

Dare saunters up to me. He pauses when we're inches apart. Rivulets of water run down his chest in interesting ways. I'm starting to wonder if actually playing ice pony polo is the best use of my time here. Maybe Dare and I could just hide out and be in bathing suits together.

Dare lifts his arm. A square of fabric sits in his hand. It's black pinnie with a blue number on it. *Thirty-Three.*

"Right," I say slowly. "If I'm going to play, I need a number."

Dare takes great care to tie it in place. The square of fabric goes on my back while there are ties which criss-cross over my chest. I think Dare brushes my skin more than is actually necessary for this particular operation.

Not that I'm complaining.

Dare slowly leans in closer.

Closer.

And our mouths meet in a fierce kiss. I can't remember wanting anything more than this in my life. Why haven't I been playing ice pony polo before?

Then it happens. The stupid whistle blows. Dare breaks the kiss and leans back. "You're on my team."

"Nuh-uh. I'm here to kick your butt."

"No doubt." He gently pulls on the strings holding my pinnie in place. "Which is why I got this on first."

"You're diabolical."

"Only in the best ways."

The whistle sounds again. We step out onto the frozen lake. All the spectators remain trapped inside their frozen donut viewing area. Sadly, I can't hear gasps of shock rise up from the audience. That said, I can see how they all freeze in place. A few flying elves forget to pump their wings and tumble right onto their asses.

It's a beautiful thing.

Dare makes a hand motion to the judge. The man rises and speaks in a magically-enhanced voice. "A new player will be added to the Royals. It's number thirty-three, Queen Calla of the Summer Realm."

Now, movement does begin. Only this time, it's in Saita's private viewing box. The queen gets up and starts pounding on the clear partition with her fists. Someone's not happy.

This just keeps getting better and better.

Dare and I step up to the edge of the playing ice. A lovely blue pony breaks through the water. She's got blue fur and matching bat wings. "Climb aboard," she says.

Ice ponies can talk. This I did not know. Although I probably should have expected it.

I swing my leg onto the saddle and grip the reins. Dare hands me a polo mallet. The judge blasts his whistle once more.

The game is on.

Now, I could have taken years to master this sport. But that really doesn't work with the whole *prankster vibe* I was searching for here. So when I cast my warming spells, I also threw in some magic to make me an ace when it comes to ice polo pony. It's really for the aesthetics of a perfect prank.

And even with my magically-enhanced play, Dare and I stay neck and neck as we hit the ball around and score points. Honestly, I'm still a little shaky on what the rules of the game are. All I know is that we won. My reward is a big hug-and-jump with Dare. And considering the water and bathing suit situation we've got going, this experience is its own kind of revelation.

The fun is cut short when Saita stomps out from her donut and approaches me and Dare.

"I take it you're joining us today for my private conversation with Dare?" asks Saita.

Dare pulls me close against his side. "That's correct."

I almost expect to see heat vapors coming off Saita's head. The woman looks that ticked off. "See you in the drawing room." Saita stomps away.

I've been to their drawing room before. It's just

another place with wooden chairs and a hearth. No one actually draws anything, which is a waste, in my opinion.

Now that Saita has put an end to *celebration time*, Dare and I magically change into our regular daywear. This could've been a sexy experience, but Saita seems cranky enough without us spending extra time to smooch or whatever. So to make things go faster, I open a ley door directly into the not-a-drawing room.

It's a shame we don't fly in through the front entrance, though. Since childhood, that's been my favorite part of the winter palace. There's something special about walking along the skinny bridge that leads to the main gate. The frozen waters below always reflect the sunbeams in a way that reminds me of a spotlight on a stage.

Since we had to skip that entrance for time, I'll draw the thing here instead.

Winter Palace

We're all alone in the drawing room. And by this, I mean it's just me, Dare, Saita… and the massive chip on the winter queen's shoulder about how I punked the polo match.

Saita wears her regular white dress. Only today, she pairs it with a deep scowl. "I'm glad you're both here."

Total lie.

"There have been rumors you both must address," continues Saita. "Word has gotten out that Dare magically created a new plague… as well as claimed responsibility for the last contagion that spread across Faerie." Saita glares at me. "Despite your action to the contrary, my spies tell me you wish to prevent this plague by kidnapping and killing my son."

I remain so calm, I should be the ice queen here.

"My own court has brought me early news of this as well," I retort. Actually, that was Poppa and Muti, not that Saita must know. "It's all a lie. Someone is trying to distract from the real threat. That's the Usurper and the Ogham sword."

Saita leans forward. Her glare gets even angrier, if that's possible. "If you place my son at risk, I'll do everything in my power to protect him."

"The same goes for you," I state. "And I think we both know who wields more magic."

Me.

A long moment passes while I hold Saita's stare without blinking. It isn't easy. In no time, my eyeballs sting like crazy. Even so, I can catch Dare in my peripheral vision. He's trying hard not to smile, the jerk.

Only, yes. This is situation is a little bit funny.

"I appreciate both of your concerns for my well being." Dare leans back in his chair. "Now, let's discuss the real reason we're here. The Usurper."

Saita looks away first. I feel like I should get a blue ribbon or something.

"What do you wish to know about the usurper?" asks Saita. The way she says those words, it's as if she's just been waiting for us to ask about the Usurper *for-EV-er.* Like she hasn't been holding back on us. What a good dodge. I'll have to practice it in my spare time. Who knows? It may come in handy someday during queen-stuff.

"How did you know about the Usurper?" asks Dare.

"Oh, that." Saita shrugs. "There wasn't a lot for the Usurper to do in the Pixieland Citadel. Let's just say the other students made it unpleasant for him there. But the Usurper was welcomed in the Summer Palace."

"And that's how you know him?" I ask.

Saita smirks. "I make it a point to know who might be enticed to share information about our summer brethren. The Usurper was useful in that way."

"The Usurper spied for us," states Dare.

Saita nods. "He provided excellent information for a long while. Then he disappeared. Bilge had already been brewing useful things for my ice garden, so I sought out our hobgoblin friend and asked him about the Usurper's welfare. That's when Bilge told me how the Usurper had already run away from the Citadel with all the supplies to find the Root Knight. The poor hobgoblin was frantic, and not without good reason. Bilge and I came up with a plan to stop the Usurper and help the Root Knight. And we'll do it again soon. Time flies when you live in Faerie."

"I don't think that plan will work twice," says Dare.

Wow, am I ever glad Dare was the one to say it. I don't

think I could handle more angry-staring with Saita. I need at least a two-minute breather.

"What are you suggesting, son?"

Dare tilts his head. "I think you know."

"I do and the answer is no," retorts Saita. "Your father is a nobody."

"Is?" Dare sits up straighter. "You normally speak of him in the past tense."

"Not sure what you mean," fibs Saita.

On second thought, I don't know if I want to pick up Saita's lying methods. I think a good liar convinces you that *they're right* and *you're wrong*. Saita just bulldozes over everyone because she's queen.

Something to contemplate later.

Saita turns to me. "Now, tell me you won't announce those decrees. At any time, the sun could shine red. We all know what that means. The harmonic equinox has arrived and with it, the Ogham sword. Everyone needs to be focused and ready to go. I knew you'd come up with some dangerous foolishness—"

"Freeing the changelings is not foolish," I state. "Neither is having a High Council that actually represents all of Faerie."

Saita looks to Dare. "Will you excuse us?" she asks sweetly. "We must have a chat, queen to queen."

Dare meets my gaze. "Calla?"

"I'm good."

Dare leaves.

Once the prince is gone, the glaring and enraged version of Saita returns. "Mark my words," says Saita. "Drop these silly decrees or you'll see what a real ruler is capable of. I have no reservations about invading the summer realm."

I rise. "I like you, Saita. And I love your son. But I'm making these decrees and if you don't approve, go on and attack." And I follow up with one last glare, just because it feels good.

Attack me? Bah!

This is the woman who lost her mind for three days because Dare broke his magical retainer. She is not going to invade my realm.

"Excuse me." I step outside, only to get enveloped in the world's best kiss.

"You love me?" asks Dare.

"You were eavesdropping, you sneak."

He winks. "Let's go scheme."

"Good idea."

Dare laces his fingers with mine. We go for a walk near the palace grounds, but that's a rather dinky space considering how the place is surrounded by a frozen lake. It does give us a chance to think through the next few days, though.

Calla and Dare's Plan

Tonight. Calla rests. I'm already starting to feel the burn from all that ice pony polo. Why did I think this was a good idea again? Oh, yeah. Bikini.

Tomorrow. Calla casts her unbreakable magic decrees. Dare looks through winter palace library for more information about the Usurper or the Ogham sword.

Day after. Calla launches her new decrees. Dare joins in on the fun.

It's a good plan.

Once I'm back home, I try to fall asleep. Not a chance. I'm so pumped for tomorrow, I can't stand it.

- Calla

Dear Diary,

When I wake up, I head straight for my new witchy workroom. At last, the place is gorgeous and fully kitted out. Cauldrons shine and potion vials gleam. All the ingredient bins are full to overflowing. Sammy's play space has plenty of roly-poly toys to keep him busy.

I get right to it.

It takes me until past midnight, but I figure out the best way to cast these magical decrees. It took a little experimentation, so I shall list my final spell here for posterity.

Creating Magical Decrees That No One Can Weasel Out Of Easily

One. Pick the right paper. Long scrolls of papyrus are clutch.

Two. Create an enchanted quill. Mine came from the tail feather of a squall bird.

Three. Find the right magical words for the decree itself. Fancier is better.

Four. Layer faerie dust atop everything.

And that's it.

Afterward, I keep unrolling the scrolls and looking them over. Simply put, I can't wait to crack these out tomorrow.

It's past 1 am when I finally try and rest. It doesn't happen. I just lie in bed and stare at the ceiling. So when my palm turns icy, I'm ready for a chat. I whisper to my hand.

"You may visit."

Seconds later, Ghost Dare appears. "How did your casting go?"

"Awesome. Everything is ready for court tomorrow."

"Just as I expected. I'll see you there." Dare brushes a ghostly kiss on my forehead and vanishes from view. After that, I zonk out right away.

- Calla

DAY 108

$\mathcal{D}$ear Diary,

It's decree day!

I'm so excited, I feel like I'm jumping out of my skin. After my experience with Lady Kae, I've learned that I must dress up for the court chamber.

Now that my nobles are sniffing around, I have to get my *fashion armor* on before I do anything as big as launching decrees.

So I magic up a few outfits before settling on something I like.

Here's what I come up with.

Decree Day

’m happy with my fashion choice. Plus, having something new to wear always gives you a secret edge. I finish off the look with my scepter, crown, and two magical decrees.

Best accessories ever.

When I stride toward the court chamber, I half-expect to see a mob of angry nobles waiting outside. But it's just Sargent Pickle and Private Elderberry, same as always.

Normally, it irritates me that my nobles avoid my official court days. Most rulers have public chambers that are packed to overflowing. Everyone wants something from the crown.

But today? I'm more blissed out than ticked off. I

know why my subjects are avoiding me. Everyone thinks I won't rule, can't last, or both.

They can kiss my butt.

All that changes today.

When I step into the chamber, I find the place is empty.

Sure, I knew Poppa, Muti, Bilge, Oinky wouldn't show. But Dare gave his word. He wouldn't break it. I try to contact hm through our ghostly connection.

Nothing happens.

I remember coming across Ivy in the hallway the other day She was so worried about Vadin. When you care about someone, it's easy to go right to the worst-case scenario.

I'm sure Dare is fine.

He has to be.

When the time comes, I give my speeches to an empty court chamber. I talk about how it's wrong to steal humans away and force them to dance and work when they don't wish it. I read the decree, cast the spell, and watch the results. Small orbs of magic fill the court chamber. Inside each sphere, I can see every changeling I just freed.

None are jumping for joy.

Most seem pretty scared.

Disappointment weighs into my bones. What did I

think? That I could just free them and they'd believe me? Most of Faerie thinks I'm a joke. These humans aren't going to risk their lives on a random spell. Even if they can leave, they're staying put.

I need to work harder on this one.

Next, I cast the spell for my new Everyone Council. Again, I speak the incantation. Once more, the chamber fills with a hundred tiny magical spheres. Inside each orb, there's the image of a single fae as they receive their golden envelope. Inside, there's an invitation to join the Everyone Council.

Unfortunately, the fae who receive my magic invites appear just as frightened as the changelings. None even open the envelope, let alone speak the magical words to accept their new jobs.

My spells are designed to remove any barriers to becoming free or joining the council. I won't turn my subjects into magical puppets. If they don't want to do something, that's fine.

It's just not what I expected.

And that feels like a total failure.

I won't lie. After casting my decrees, I spend some quality time moping in my bedroom. And when I finally do fall asleep, my mind is haunted by darkness.

- Calla

My Dream

I dream that Dare and I step into the main ballroom of the winter palace. Both of us wear our royal and formal best.

Saita watches as we enter, her face the very definition of joyful. All my friends and family are in attendance as well: Poppa, Muti, Bilge, Oinky, Ivy, and even Vadin. They're all as excited as Saita.

With light hearts and smiling faces, Dare and I stride through the crowd. Our subjects part for us as we march along. Members of my new Everybody Council all wave their golden invites at me with pride. Changelings and elves stand beside each other without fear or anger.

Music strikes up. Dare and I move out onto the dance floor. I wrap my arms around his neck, loving the warm feel of his skin. A voice whispers in my ear.

"It's all a lie. Dare is dead."

I open my eyes and find that Dare is now a skinless corpse. The voice who spoke to me is another skeleton, only this one is dressed as a jester.

Panic streams through me. The walls of the ballroom heave and twist in that terrifying way that only true nightmares can manage.

I awaken with a gasp. After that nightmare, I know one thing for certain.

Dare is in danger.

- Calla

DAY 109

*D*ear Diary,

When I wake up today, I'm in a total panic. I let myself wallow in the sensation for a few five minutes.

Then I get to finding Dare.

I try my ghost connection again. There's no response. Reaching down, I pull up a floorboard. Ley lines glimmer underneath. Pulling these up, I create a door to the winter palace.

My spell gets blocked. This has only happened a few times before. Mostly, that happens when I try to open a portal directly into Mother's castle. But that's to be expected. My mother is the guru of ley magic. I'm sure she can block my junior spells in her sleep.

So who is sealing me away from the winter palace?

I try to more ley doors. Each time, I create the portal a little farther from the winter palace itself. If my guess is right, this blocking spell has some kind of perimeter limit. I don't need to appear right in the drawing room of the castle. All I require is to get closer than half-way across Faerie.

At last, I'm able to open a ley door that actually works. My heart pounds with such vigor, I can feel my pulse in my throat.

When I step through the portal, I can't believe what I find.

The winter palace is a wreck.

The ice lake surrounding the castle has been hollowed out. Where once was frozen water, there's now just the stinking slop at the bottom of the lake.

I've seen the winter palace so often, I could draw it from memory. In fact, I did exactly that not too long ago. And now, it's a ruin.

Winter Palace

I slog across the lake bed. In my rush to get to the palace, I didn't cast any spells for warmth, so this is a chilly walk at best. Even so, the cold doesn't matter. I just have to get to the front gate. A single thought keeps echoing through my head.

Find Dare.

At last, I hike up the columns to the walkway that connects to the front gate. Not so long ago, this was one of my favorite spots in Faerie. Now it's burned out. Charcoal blasts mark the once-white granite. Claw marks are everywhere. Some part of me knows this means something. It's a clue.

I can't focus on any of that now, though. It's all I can do to keep moving forward. My fingertips have turned blue. I can't stop my teeth from chattering. It's like living a nightmare.

Keep walking.

At last, I hobble toward the front gate. In my mind, I know this isn't a dream. It still feels that way, though. Because as I close in on the entrance, I find a familiar figure standing there.

Saita.

"You!" she gestures to me. "Returning to the scene of the crime, eh? You took your fire drakes, blasted my castle apart, and killed my son!"

I can only stand in place and shiver. "No, that wasn't me. Where's the prince?"

"You took him!" screeches Saita. "Someone told you he needed to die in order to stop another plague and you believed it. Worse yet, you lied to me that you loved my boy… while it was *you* who took his life!"

"Dare is dead." I try the words out on my tongue. They don't feel real.

"Guards!" cries Saita. "Arrest her! Throw her in the dungeons. Alert Lady Kae to take the throne."

For what feels like hours, I've shuffled along in a daze. Saita's last words snap me out of my funk and how. On reflex, I kneel down. Pressing my hands to the ground, I get ready to pull up ley lines and make my escape.

"I used a wand to block your ley power here," snarls Saita. "I thought it would protect my son. But it didn't stop your fire drakes, now did it?"

"I don't have any fire drakes," I murmur. "They don't serve the summer realm."

"Liar!" cries Saita. "Release the ice dragons! Catch her!"

Unlike fire drakes, ice dragons actually do what Saita orders. I must get out of here and fast. Without a ley line for escape, I do the next best thing: unfurl my wings and take to the skies. I pump with all my strength while aiming for the spot where I created my last ley door.

As I speed along, the beat of heavy wings sounds behind me. Ice dragons. They roar and release columns of frozen water all around. I'm hit in my right leg and left arm. Still, I don't stop.

Finally, I spy my old ley door up ahead on the lake floor. Fortunately, it's sitting right where I left it. Using one last burst of energy, I fly right through the portal, using my head and good shoulder as a battering ram. The wooden entrance shatters around me. Hundreds of splinters pierce my skin. As I pass through, I picture the only place I can go where I may actually find help.

The ley castle.

And I hope my magic will take me there. The next

thing I know, I'm slamming onto a cold floor. My ears ring from the crack of my own skull whacking against a rock. I struggle to open my eyes, but it's no use.

Darkness fills my mind and I lose consciousness.

- Calla

Dear Diary,

Today, I wake up to find myself lying on a comfy cot in a small blue room. There's an open pit in the center of the floor and a matching hole in the ceiling. Ley lines flow upward between the two spots. That means only one thing.

I'm in the ley castle. I made it.

Some ley lines connect Earth to Faerie. Those are found underground. But the lines here? These control the past, present, and future. This castle is filled with similar chambers. Mother visits them, sifts through possible timelines, and prunes out the ones that don't work.

And Mother is before me now.

The Ley Queen looks as she always does: an ethereal

beauty with a ballet dancer's body and long blue hair. She wears a sapphire-colored robe.

With careful movements, Mother brushes her fingertips across the many ley lines that flow before her. Every so often, she pulls out a single thread and tosses it aside.

Today, she doesn't perform that work alone. Father stands beside her.

Unlike the Ley Queen, King Tristan has changed a lot since I last saw him. Which makes sense. After all, Dad had been trapped in an enchanted sleep for ages— that's bound to do a number on your muscle tone and personal hygiene.

But since then, Father's had some time to cast spells and get back to his regular elfy self. He has strawberry blond hair that's cropped short. His body is lean and strong; the kind of physique that you'd see on a human swimmer.

Best of all, my parents work in concert with each other as they sort through the upward flow of ley lines. It had never occurred to me that anyone who isn't a ley elemental could do this kind of work. Good to know it's possible. You never know what will happen with me and Dare.

Dare. The name makes me sit bolt upright.

Is he dead? Safe?

My parents hear my movement and turn to face me. It's Mother who speaks first. "You look better."

Father beams. "My lovely Calla."

I rub my temples with my fingertips. Turns out, sitting up that quickly is a bad idea. Mother glide-walks up to me. With graceful movements, she sets the back over her hand against my forehead.

"Are you feeling ill?" she asks. "Do you need some water?"

"I'll get her some elf crackers." Father focuses on me. "I heard you love those."

"No, I don't need any of that. I'm here because I can't find Dare. Saita says he's dead and I killed him."

Mother sits down beside me on the cot. She pats my hand. "Don't worry. We know you're innocent. You'd never murder someone just to stop a plague."

"Exactly," adds Father. "Plus, no one has even died from this disease yet. It's all very shady, if you asked me."

"I'm glad you believe in me," I say quickly. "But my guilt or innocence isn't important here. I must know—"

Mother pats my hand once more. "Oh, your inno- cence is very important to us. Especially since false beliefs about your guilt forced you to get injured."

Father nods. "You've been recovering for two days."

My mouth falls open. "Two days?"

Now it's Mother's turn to nod. "Yes, we've been

casting healing spells on you all this time. I'm glad to report that you're fully recovered."

I pinch the bridge of my nose. "Look, I don't mean to be obsessive here, but I really must find Dare. Have either of you—"

"Elf crackers!" interrupts Father. "That's definitely what you need."

I narrow my eyes and scan both of my parents from head to toe. I don't know either of them well, but certain interactions are so obvious, you don't need to know someone forever in order to understand what's happening.

"You guys are stalling on me," I declare. "I won't drop this. Whatever happened to Dare, I can handle it. I just need the truth."

Mother rises and returns to her work at sorting through ley lines. "Dare's fate is a mystery."

I stand up. "What do you mean, it's a mystery? You're the Ley Queen. It's your job to sort through time and space. I can't believe you don't know what happened. Can you at least tell me if Dare's alive?"

Mother stays silent as she goes about her work. I round on father. "What about you? I saw how you manipulate ley lines, the same as mother. Do you know anything?"

Father crosses the room. He wears the tunic and loose

pants that are common for summer elves. The bright silk shimmies with each step. It strikes me that it's such a beautiful way to move when he's being so horrible right now.

I march closer to Father. "Well?"

Father focuses on the ley lines like his life depends on it. Then he repeats the same thing as Mom. "Dare's fate is a mystery."

For a long minute, it's all I can do to stare between my parents in disbelief. All this time, I thought they were canoodling on their second honeymoon. Instead, they're standing around, sorting ley lines, and not answering basic questions from their only child.

My gaze locks on the exit door. I've spent time in the ley castle before. Outside this chamber, there's a hallway lined with doors. And behind each of those entrances, there's another ley line room just like this one.

Well, I'm a ley elemental, too. I don't need to wait for anyone to get me answers. I'll find them myself.

I march out the exit and into the nearest ley room. Once inside, I slam the door and cast the biggest, nastiest locking spell I can think of.

Then I turn to the flow of ley lines in the center of the room. Unlike the last chamber, these blue cords flow from the ceiling into the floor, waterfall-style. Does that mean something?

One way to find out.

With cautious steps, I inch closer to the cascade of ley lines. Pounding sounds behind me as my parents try to break into the room.

"Stop!" cries Mother. "It isn't safe!"

"You'll kill yourself!" yells Father.

And maybe they're both right. At this point, I don't care. If I want answers, I must take risks. Reaching forward, I grab the nearest ley line. It burns my fingers. On reflex, my arm snaps back.

The pounding grows louder. I also hear the low murmur of Father's voice. He's casting a spell. Both of my parents are excellent magic users. I won't have long before they break in and stop me.

Screw it.

Reaching forward, I grab two full handfuls of ley lines. Pain sears up my arms. My entire body feels as if it's on fire.

I've never used these kind of ley lines before, but I have cast plenty of spells. When it comes to traditional magic, everything is about intent. Closing my eyes, I make my wishes clear in my mind.

Show me Dare.

Pictures flash in my head. I see a deserted road that cuts through a wasteland of scrub brush. The trail ends at a rickety house. The front door hangs off one hinge. Most windows are smashed in.

I grab onto the ley lines more tightly. Fresh pain sears through me, but I grit my teeth and focus on the scene in my mind.

In my thoughts, I fly up the broken front steps of the house and into what was once a living room. Six humans stand in a semicircle that faces the corner. All of them wield guns. Behind them, I count a dozen winter fae in their leather armor. Each of them holds a wand. Everyone points their weapon of choice at the same corner of the room.

Which is where Dare stands.

I exhale. *He's alive!* And based on the fact that there are armed humans nearby, he's also on Earth.

The winter elves are the real giveaway. Chances are, this is all Saita's doing. She wants Dare safe from the Usurper and from me. If that means fake-kidnapping her own son and jailing him on Earth, so be it.

This will make future family holidays awkward, but there's no point worrying about it now.

I'm setting Dare free.

I keep my tight grip on the ley lines. Behind me, the door creaks on its hinges.

In my vision, I float closer to Dare. We've spent so many years communicating with our astral selves. This has to work one more time. With all my will, I call upon the bond between us.

See me.

Dare looks up. Our gazes lock. A snarky grin rounds his mouth. He looks perfectly healthy and unhurt. If anything, standing in a corner doing nothing all day would only bore the prince to death.

Take my hands.

I press my arms forward, hoping that somehow I use the ley lines to connect to Dare. In the house on earth, Dare reaches out as well. At first, I sense no movement on the ley lines.

Then the blue cords crackle with magic and life. I feel the familiar pressure of Dare's grip against my own.

Fort a second, all of Dare's jailers stare in shock. What a sight we must make. I'm a floating torso who just appeared in their ruined cabin.

Then they get rowdy. All of Dare's guards decide that I'm a threat. Guns and wands get pointed in my direction.

Dare loses his mind.

"Not Calla!" he cries.

There's a flurry of kicks and lunges as Dare knocks out every guard in the room. Then he turns and grasps my hands once more.

Bracing myself, I lean backward, hauling Dare out of

the shower of ley lines and into the chamber. The prince lands right beside me.

We share a smile and a kiss. It's a lovely moment until my parents knock the door down. I turn toward the waterfall of ley magic.

"Jump!" I cry.

Together, Dare and I leap into the pit of magic. As we fall, I picture our destination. It feels as if we tumble for hours before landing in a crouch.

And we're still holding hands.

I can't help but laugh hysterically. It's a little weird, but so is this entire situation. We've landed back in my bedroom in the summer palace.

"I have a lot to tell you," I say, my voice rough.

"As do I."

My legs turn watery beneath me. I hadn't realized what grabbing the ley lines was really doing to my body. "I think I'm going to pass out now."

Dare scoops me into his arms before my head hits the floor again. That's got to be a good thing. For the second time in three days, I lose consciousness.

Only this time, I do so with a smile.

- Calla

*D*ear Diary,

When I open my eyes, I find myself in the comfort of my own bed. A very warm and snuggly Dare lies behind me, his hand draped over my stomach.

"Calla?" he whispers. "Are you awake?"

I nod. "How long was I out for this time?"

"Two days."

"Same as last time. At least, I'm consistent."

"Your parents covered you with very intricate healing spells. Most of the work was done for me. I just needed to add in extra power to keep the magic strong."

"I guess that's nice."

"But?"

"I escaped to the ley castle like a superhero and they

wouldn't do anything to help me find you. I plan to pretend they don't exist."

"When did you come up with this scheme?"

"Just now."

"And how long do you want to keep it up?"

"Two, maybe three months."

"I'll join you. I already have no idea who my father is, so that part will be easy. And at this point, it would be lovely to think there's no Saita in my life."

I hiss in a worried breath. "I almost hate to ask this, but what did she do?"

"I found her plans for hiding me and framing you. Honestly, Calla. Destroying my family palace… faking my murder… and framing you for the deed? That's not just outrageous; it's foolhardy. If you want to launch a fake attack on your own castle, don't ask half the faerie population of fire drakes to help. They're total blabbermouths."

I narrow my eyes and process this news. "So a fire drake told you?"

"Technically, a fire drake told his cleaning lady who also tidies up for the chief of my secret police."

"Wait. Fire drakes have cleaning ladies?"

"Sure. Can you imagine them trying to straighten up with those claws?"

"Okay, I get that. When you were taken?"

"I confronted Saita about her plans to *protect me.*" There's a definite sarcastic tone as dare says the words, *protect me.* "Throughout the whole conversation, Saita was very calm and reasonable. She agreed I was right and promised to cease her schemes immediately. Then she chucked a vial of sleeping potion in my face."

"Ouch. I thought my birth parents were cold."

"When I woke up, I found myself in a shack on Earth and surrounded by an obnoxious number of guards. I saw your torso made from blue ley lines. You know the rest."

There's a lot more stuff to chat about, but my eyelids suddenly feel like they weigh a ton. I decide to close my eyes for just a second and end up falling right asleep.

- Calla

Dear Diary,

Dare insists I stay in bed again today. While I snuggle under the covers, he sits nearby and reads me hobgoblin history (my favorite). I'm also spoon-fed ice cream.

Now, this is what queen life should all be about.

I want to give Dare a tour of my witchy workroom. But I keep falling asleep before I get around to it.

- Calla

*D*ear Diary,

Today I finally give dare a tour of my witchy workroom. We totally broke in the bouncy castle, too. That really is one of my best ideas. Plus, Sammy loves his play area. There's nothing better than a happy scepter.

Since we were in the room where I cast my magical decrees, I also recount my Changeling-Council Plan failure. Dare says, *it's not how you fall down, it's how you get up.*

And maybe, I will regroup. Later.

I take some time and design a new outfit. After all, near-death experiences require wardrobe additions. My creation looks remarkably like my regular mini-dress, only there are sequins and a tube top. Big improvement.

My very important fashion drawing is on the next page.

- Calla

My New Dress

DAY 116

Dear Diary,

When I wake up today, I feel like myself again. Finally. Energy streams through my limbs. Classic interests return. For instance, I've a healthy desire for both Pixie-Os and to punch the Usurper in the face.

Another bonus: I have a very nice snuggle partner who now lies nose-to-nose with me. Dare also runs his fingertips along the neckline of my nightie. What a nice way to start the morning.

For a minute, I just soak in the sight of Dare. I love how the morning light plays across the sharp lines of the prince's face. Dare is so perfect, it's as if he's carved from marble versus made from flesh and blood.

Every nerve ending my body goes on alert as I notice

something unexpected. The light streaming into my room now changes in hue.

It's turning red.

Some part of me knows what this means—the harmonic equinox is here. But a small corner of my heart says this could be a mistake. Kicking off my covers, I rush out the balcony. Dare steps along at my side.

I stand on the balcony, gripping the railing like my life depends on it. A magical haze hangs over the sun. I look directly into the light.

Sure enough, the sun now swirls with shades of red. It's both beautiful beyond belief... and scary as all get out.

I'm drawing this scene for certain.

Equinox

*B*elow me, my guards stare up at the same view.

Captain Solei marches closer. "What is it, your Majesty?"

"It's something called the harmonic equinox."

"Magic?" she asks.

"Yes," I reply. "But it's nothing that threatens the castle. I'll be gone for the day."

This is a little bit of fae double-speak. The castle will be fine. Everyone who lives in it and my realm? Maybe not so much. But there's no point getting my warriors all cranked up. The army can't take down the Usurper. If this is their last day, they may as well be calm through it.

Solei removes her golden helmet. Her long white-blonde hair falls free. For the first time, I get a good look at her face. A long scar trails from her right eye down to her chin. No doubt about it. Solei has seen some tough fights.

Concern now shines in Solei's blue eyes. Knowing this is warrior has seen battle—and that she took the time to show me this fact—makes her anxiety carry extra weight. "Be safe, your Majesty."

Dare sets his hand at my waistline. "She'll be protected," he declares.

Solei scans Dare carefully. It's no secret that I'm not a major warrior in the muscly sense. I fight with magic. She nods and resets her helm. "Good."

As I watch Solei march off into the woods, it strikes me that my guards were comfortable freaking out about nothing. Now, they have a warriors' sense that something terrible is coming... and they transform into a real fighting unit. The fighters move in precise formation as they take their positions on the perimeter of the castle. All are focused on their duty.

Somehow, that makes me more concerned, not less. What does it say that a seasoned warrior knows the challenges ahead without knowing anything specific about the Usurper?

Dare rests his hands on my shoulders. With gentle

movements, he guides my body so we stand facing each other with our chests a few inches apart.

Our gazes lock. All the intensity in the universe now shines in the prince's eyes. There's excitement there, as well as an appetite for adventure. His inner spark is contagious. Part of my soul captures this moment.

That time Dare and I found the Ogham sword after years of searching.

"What do you say, Pirate Calla? Ready to magically set our treasure map?"

I take in a deep breath. Strength flows into me along with the fresh air. I set my hands atop the prince's. "So ready."

"Let's make some magic."

Although my guards carefully avoid directly staring at me and Dare, there's no doubt the warriors closely watch our every move. If we're about to cast a spell to find the Ogham sword, we don't need a pack of warriors gaining the information.

I tilt my head toward my bedroom and raise my brows. The statement is there, if unspoken.

We should go back inside.

Dare nods. Together, the prince and I march back into my bedroom. Once there, our actions are protected by the pack of obfuscation spells I cast on this place.

Time for our final adventure to begin.

Dare raises his hands. An orb of power materializes between his palms. Countless particles of light and power dance within the sphere. I've never seen more energy in a casting.

Dare separates his arms; the sphere breaks free. The orb swoops around my room in a great circle before spiraling down toward the floor.

Sammy gets interested. Normally, my scepter likes to sleep all day. Not now. Sammy slowly rolls out from his favorite snoozing spot under my bed. Although my magical buddy doesn't have eyes, I can still tell when Sammy watches something carefully. Right now, Sammy is soaking in the sight of another supernatural round thing as it puts on a show.

With a great flash of light, Dare's power orb crashes onto the center of the floor. From there, it expands and contracts until it takes the shapes of a semi-transparent mountain range. My breath catches.

With slow steps, I circle around the three-dimensional image that now covers my bedroom floor. I've seen this particular landscape before. "That's Hyperborea."

The humans have the Himalayas; my summer realm contains Hyperborea. It's the largest and tallest mountain range around. There's one big difference between these peaks and their human counterparts, though. Hyperborea sports mountains that tower into the heights of cold and ice. Yet between each peak, there's a deep valley which is rich in sunshine and warmth.

It makes perfect sense. If I were going to hide the Ogham tree, I'd definitely chuck it into one of the many valleys that pockmark Hyperborea.

Dare slowly steps around the miniature mountain range. One particular valley pulses with bright red light. Dare points to the spot. "Here. That's where the Ogham tree will reappear."

"Right." Stepping closer, I examine at the spot in question. It resembles every other valley in the Hyperborea.

My mind sorts through everything I've learned about what happens next. None of this is new, but facing the fact that will come to pass in a matter of minutes? I want to ensure I have it down cold.

"The red light of the harmonic equinox will grow brighter," I begin. Without consciously willing it, my voice carries a low and reverent tone. "The most intense spot will be in this valley. When the equinox reaches its peak, the Ogham tree will reappear." I reach forward until my fingertips touch the bright representation of the valley. Red lights and patterns shift across my skin.

Dare picks up the narrative. "And once the oak appears in the valley, so will the Usurper. That's when the real search will begin."

Images from the past fill my mind. I recall what happened when Dare and I used the enchanter's wisher. We saw the first time the Usurper sought out the Ogham sword. I sort through the memory one last time, carefully.

When I speak again, my voice carries the same quiet sense of purpose. "The last time this happened, the Usurper stepped from tree to tree. Each time, he set his hands on the bark and spoke the incantation. Then he killed countless innocent lives."

"We stick to our plan," says Dare. "That means arriving first with better weapons and magic."

"Agreed." I pull up a haze of faerie dust and command it to get me ready. The sparkling bits settle onto my nightie, changing the garment into my newly-designed mini-dress. Next, I wave to Sammy, who bounces closer. "In my pocket, buddy." Sammy shrinks down to the size of a gumball and hides himself away. I consider casting myself some breakfast, but toss the idea aside. I'm too cranked up to eat.

For his part, Dare quickly summons fresh orbs of power. Just as with me, the magic settles onto his clothes. In this case, Dare's loose sleep pants transform into battle armor. The prince casts more magical spheres. These solidify into various long swords and daggers. Somehow, Dare finds room for them all under his heavy fur cloak.

"I'm ready," declares Dare.

"Same here."

Dare gives me the side-eye. "Not quite." He pulls up another sphere of magic and sends it toward me. The sparkling orb soaks into my chest. The impact doesn't hurt, though. If anything, it tickles.

White magic spreads across my body. The power quickly solidifies into my own set of leather body armor. Pink, of course.

I scope myself out in a nearby full-length mirror. "Much better." Dare even cast me a little pocket that's perfect for Sammy. "Thank you."

"Any time."

We share another long look. This is it. Per our plan, we must get to the tree first and with the best weapons. The preparation part of the day is over.

It's time to go.

Here's where my ley powers come in. Kneeling down, I pull up a floorboard and another ley lines from underneath. Standing again, I twist the cords into the rough shape of an arched doorway. The ropes of blue energy solidify into a door that's covered in bark.

That's perfect for the Ogham.

With our weapons and magic in hand, we step through the portal and into Hyperborea.

Hyperborea

Dare and I step through the portal and into an untouched stretch of oak forest. There don't seem to be any fae around. Good.

The crimson light is stronger here than back at the palace. It's a little gross to write this down, but it looks as if everything is covered in blood. Not that it is *really* is, but having the illusion doesn't set a good tone for the day.

There's nothing to be done about it, though. Changing the effect of the light isn't our first goal here.

Finding the Ogham tree is.

Dare and I make our way through the oak forest. As we step along, we carefully watch for any sign that the crimson light is growing more intense.

Are we heading to the spot where the Ogham tree grows?

Or are we already there?

After some careful roaming, we figure out that the red light is focused on a circle of space that's about a fae league across. In human terms, that's about a mile wide. It doesn't sound like a lot of space, but when you have to touch every tree in it? Trust me, it's a total pain.

We brought along a few potions and finder spells for just such an occasion. As we feared, none of them work. There's nothing to it but to go back to the original plan from when Dare and I were kids.

Touch trees, say the spell, and hope for the best.

We test about thirty oaks. Nothing happens each time. It's super nerve-wracking. At any moment, the harmonic equinox could reach its peak.

When that happens, we won't be the only ones searching.

Rustling erupts from a nearby patch of ground. Dare and I go on alert. Both of us cast obfuscation spells as we wait to see what's coming. In other words, we're both in ghost mode now.

Little piles of soil churn up from the earth. The scent of leaves and fresh dirt fill the air. Excitement zings through my body.

Please, let the Ogham tree rise up now.

And as it turns out, I am correct. *But only partly.* Because something does indeed break free from the soil.

Sadly, it's the Usurper.

Inch by inch, a dark figure presses up from the broken ground. He looks just like he did when we magically visited the past: a dark sorcerer with six arms who wears a hooded cloak.

Before, it was just me, Dare, and the hope of finding a magical oak. Now we've got some competition. My pulse speeds.

The Usurper immediately floats over to the nearest tree. Setting his hands against the trunk, the sorcerer recites the ancient spell.

Root Knight, Root Knight
Holding your magic inside this tree
Root Knight, Root Knight
Open and give your sword to me

My breath catches. This can't be happening so soon. If the Usurper finds the Ogham sword first, then things become much more tricky.

Long seconds tick by. The Usurper hovers in mid-air, unmoving. Yet the tree doesn't open. No Root Knight appears. A weight of worry seeps away from my shoulders. We still have time.

The Usurper floats over to the next oak in line. A memory appears. Again, this is exactly what the Usurper did the first time he went after the Ogham. Dare and I had worried about this. The Usurper is a sorcerer with forty-thousand years to scheme. In all that time, it's likely that he'd figure out some magic to find the tree more quickly. Doesn't look like it, though. The Usurper is floating from oak to oak, just the same as he did last time.

Fresh rustling sounds echo through the forest. While staying in our ghostly forms, Dare and I run off after the noise. As we speed along, I wonder who we will find. Saita? Oinky? Bilge?

It's none of those.

Because if I thought running across the Usurper was a shock, then this is far worse.

The noisy traveler is none other than Jolly. My one-time home tree is marching through the woods, naiad style. He steps out from the thick of the forest and into a massive clearing. Now, it's easy to detect that Poppa, Muti, and Saita are all flying along nearby. Meanwhile, Bilge and Oinky are carried within Jolly's branch-like arms.

Oh, no.

Again, I can't help but notice how Jolly's root legs gleam with that particular sapphire hue.

Ley magic.

It's the same power that appeared on bark of the Root Knight himself. It's that magic which spawned the Ogham sword as well.

And it's the identical energy in me.

That fact spins through me in new ways. Old memories appear. Fresh connections form. Multiple strands of thought whip through my mind, the many threads twisting together into a heavy cord of realization.

I stop in place, unable to move closer to Jolly. Ghost Dare pauses as well. Now we stand on one side of the huge clearing while everyone else waits on the opposite edge.

Ghost Dare rests his hand on my shoulder. "What's wrong, Calla?"

"The Ogham sword," I begin. "I know where it is."

Ghost Dare looks between me and my home tree. "You can't mean…" He leaves the thought out there.

"The Ogham is inside Jolly," I confirm. "Always has been. Poppa and Muti have been caretakers of the weapon for forty-thousand years. That's why my birth parents trusted them with raising me. Poppa and Muti are exceptionally good at hiding incredibly powerful magic."

With that thought in mind, I'm ready to move into action once more. While making myself visible again, I rush across the clearing, careful to make the most direct path toward Jolly. Once I'm close enough, I wave while speaking in an urgent whisper.

"You have to stop," I warn. "Turn back. The Usurper is close. You're the only tree that's walking. That makes it too easy for the Usurper to find what he seeks."

At this point, I'd hoped everyone would run away. That's not what happens. Jolly keeps walking toward the absolute center point of the round clearing.

It's Saita who makes a detour. Dare's mother swoops down toward me with her arms raised and nails bared. And she isn't flying in to compare manicures. Based on the way her face contorts with rage? She's ready to scratch my eyes out.

Ugh.

And I should have planned for this. Sadly, I'd been so focused on the Usurper, I hadn't thought about Saita. Turns out, I don't need to worry. Dare steps right between me and his mother. Essentially, the prince uses his own body to block her attack.

A few years from my face, Saita stops and hovers in place. The only thing keeping her from me is Dare. When he speaks, the prince's tone drips with menace.

"Don't," he commands.

Saita lowers her arms and wings her way back to Jolly.

I shouldn't take pleasure in that sight. Nope. Not a bit. But I am fae. We're kind of terrible. So I do enjoy this moment a little.

Bilge waves to me from Jolly's branches. "Calla, you're here!"

Shock prickles across my skin. Bilge did not just do that.

"Calla, Calla, CALLLLLLLLLLAAAAAA!"

And that's Bilge. Again.

My heart sinks. *Did Bilge really just yell to me? Why not take out an advertisement, too?*

I look to Dare. "Oh, no."

Dare shakes his head. "I'd cast a silencer spell, but it would just waste magical energy. If the Usurper can hear us, then it's happened already."

Bilge slaps Jolly's branchy arms. The oak tree sets his hobgoblin passenger on the ground. Once he's on the green, Bilgy toddle-races toward us while continuing to speak at a really inappropriate volume.

"Jolly can't turn back," cries Bilge. "This is what our oak friend is magically compelled to do. Everything will be fine. We went through this before, remember? You'll see. Just stay out of the way and all will be well." Bilge snaps his fingers. "I have an idea, why don't you—"

I raise my pointer finger. "If you say, *play a prank,* then I'll punch you in the nose."

Bilge presses his mouth shut tight. At least in this, *someone's* listening to me.

Jolly reaches the absolute center of the round clearing. Then he stops. A great column of red light shoots down from the skies, bathing Jolly in the darkest and —*much as I hate to say it*—bloodiest light yet.

Okay, Bilge made too much noise. But on the positive side, we found the Ogham oak. Now it's just a matter of getting the sword first. Dare has the same idea. We don't need to have a long chat; our plan was laid out days ago.

Dare and I release our wings and fly off at top speed. No matter what, we must reach Jolly first.

Twenty yards.

Ten.

Five.

All of a sudden, the Usurper speeds into the clearing. No matter how quickly Dare and I fly, the Usurper goes faster. I've seen compounded speed spells before. This is the most layered one I've ever witnessed.

Guess I know what the Usurper did all those years with his time and magic. My heart tumbles. What a disaster.

For his part, Bilge is beaming from ear to ear. Poppa and Muti watch from a safe distance while frantically waving me over to their side. And Saita lurks along the forest edge. Talk about a misguided sense of protective instinct. If Dare needed any help in getting not-killed by the Usurper, now would be the time to act.

The Usurper sets his palms against Jolly's bark.

A frantic thought overtakes my mind. If nothing else, I can push the Usurper away from my beloved Jolly. I fly closer but get stopped mid-air.

Slam!

Dare and I run smack into an invisible wall. Looks like a speed spell wasn't the only thing the Usurper brought along.

We must break through.

Dare and I strike the barrier, cast spells, and even use a few choice swear words. Nothing helps.

We can't get any closer to Jolly.

The moment seems to freeze in time. For days, I've been trying to grasp at memories that have stayed just out of reach. Now those recollections appear at last. And I know one thing with perfect clarity.

This isn't going to be anything like the last time the Ogham sword appeared.

The Usurper speaks the incantation once more.

Root Knight, Root Knight
Holding your magic inside this tree
Root Knight, Root Knight

Open and give your sword to me

The bark glistens and splits. A figure steps out from within Jolly.

It's Dame Guinevere. And she's holding the Ogham sword.

More memories appear with perfect clarity. Guinevere was the girl who would appear to me in my room growing up. Which means Guinevere lied about being part of the Errigal. There's no way Guinevere joined a band of roving outlaws. She's been living inside Jolly's trunk.

Now Guinevere and the Usurper stand face to face. The evil sorcerer holds out his arms. "Don't bother with the words about charity and life. Just hand over the Ogham, Root Knight."

"As you command," says Guinevere. And she plunges the blade right through the Usurper's chest. "You murdered my brother. I was his second in command. It was my fate to hide in the forest and watch you slaughter my sibling from afar."

When I traveled through time, I saw that murder as well. Back then, I remember someone lurking in the forest. Yet there was so much happening with the Usurper, I didn't pay close enough attention.

"On the day of my brother's death, I vowed to take

revenge." Guinevere twists the blade. "None of your bloodline deserves to live."

Guinevere's plan comes into full clarity now. She's about to speak the incantation to wipe out not just the Usurper, but everyone of his kind.

And the Usurper is an elf.

She'll kill us all.

I pound on the barrier separating me from Guinevere. "Don't do it!" I cry. "Stop!"

If Guinevere hears my pleading, she doesn't show it. Instead, she twists the blade even deeper as she begins the final spell.

One for many,
Magic of plenty.
Make me death and bones!

Just as before, blue light shines on the Usurper. He's not the only one, though. The magical brightness appears on me, Dare and Saita as well. The prince's mother tumbles to the ground. Where once flew a mighty queen, now there's only a pile of bones.

At the same time, power flows from across Faerie and goes right into Guinevere. It's just like what happened before with the folly lambs. Only unlike the Usurper, Guinevere doesn't end up damaged after she takes in all the extra energy. Which makes sense. After all, she's a ley elemental taking in more of her own magic.

Pain slices through me, like a thousand knives carving my flesh at once. I crumple over. Hurt and ache infest every cell in my body, yet I don't die. Waves of agony radiate through me with such force, I can't even think straight. For a moment, I don't understand why I'm still alive.

Then the truth appears in my mind. I'm half ley elemental. Right now, only my summer self side is dying.

Bilge scurries over to Saita's bones. Kneeling over her corpse, the hobgoblin lets out a long wail. Poppa and Muti cower by Bilge's side.

Oinky loses his mind.

The mini pig makes a straight path for Guinevere. And in doing so, Oinky reveals a major strategic bonus.

There's no more Usurper.

Which means there's no more force field keeping me away from the Ogham sword.

I picture all my subjects across the realm. Moments ago, all of them were alive with their own worries and hopes. Now every last one is dead. None deserve this. Even Saita. After all, her only goal is to protect Dare.

Saita went about it in the wrong way, but her heart was in the right place. Mostly.

Which brings me to Dare.

What was once my best friend and first love is now a lump of heavy furs strewn across the forest floor. My gaze swings back to the Ogham sword. That distinctive shade of blue glimmers across the blade. Ley magic.

Memories of the ley castle fill my mind. I recall how my parents pounded on the door while I pulled Dare out of the ley pit. I had no idea what I was doing then. Everything seemed to work out anyway.

An idea appears. I'll just grab the sword and tap into its inner ley energy. There must be some way to use its magic to fix everything.

If not, then I'll just kill Guinevere and call it a day.

I nod once, my plan set.

In my mind, I stalk over to Guinevere like a badass. In reality, I'm half hunched over with a seriously melted face. It's like I fell out of a bad zombie movie.

"Hand over the Ogham," I order. "I must save my people."

Guinevere frowns. "How are you alive?"

"I'm only half-elf, don't you remember?"

"Right."

One thing I'll say for Guinevere, she's not a girl who

does what you'd expect. Suddenly, Guinevere lunges at me, pinning my back to the ground.

Normally, I'd put up more of a fight—or any, really—but I'm half-zombie at this point. Twitching is really my only defense. And don't get me started on my magic. Fae stuff is what I really know how to wield. That side of me is toast. The only thing I have left is my elemental ley magic. And that's definitely in *fake it til you make it* mode.

Which brings me back to my somewhat pathetic fight with Guinevere. She sits on my chest while holding the Ogham sword above her head. Not sure what kind of killing blow that will deal, but it'll certainly hurt.

"You want the Ogham sword?" asks Guinevere. "I thought you understood. My brother was the one who revered life. I plan to wipe it out in a way that's far worse than the Usurper ever could."

"Got it," I snark. "Thanks for sharing."

When you're half-dead and about to get killed by a psychopathic tree girl with a magic sword, then sassing off is a totally acceptable battle tactic.

"This is where you die," adds the very blabby Guinevere.

A tall figure rises up behind her. It's Dare. His skin has a strange hue to it. And I've never seen him look this ripped. He wields a longsword in each hand like it's nothing at all.

"Looks like I'm only half elf as well," announces Dare. He brings the longswords down in a scissor-like motion. One second, Guinevere has a head. The next moment, I vow to burn my outfit if I ever live through this.

Dare flicks Guinevere off me like she weighs nothing. Whatever Dare's daddy-half might be, losing his elf nature has temporarily made the prince stronger, not weaker.

Dare lifts me from the ground and sets me on my feet so quickly, I'm surprised I don't dry heave. He then plucks the sword from the ground and offers it to me. "From what you were saying the Guinevere, it seemed as if you have an idea on how to fix all this."

"I do, as a matter of fact."

"Of course," Dare winks.

The ground rumbles. This time, it's a deep groan of many taloned feet slapping on the earth. Dare and I have heard this noise before, back when we were visiting the Talking Desert. Sure enough, a herd of fire drakes appear through line the trees. The vizier jumps out from the group.

"We helped stage a fake abduction of Prince Dare," cries the vizier. "Saita promised us treasure."

I roll my eyes. "Well, Saita's a little dead right now.

Give me a minute to maybe bring her back and you two can talk."

The skies darken. An ethereal chill takes over the atmosphere. A dozen ice dragons swoop down to land in the clearing. The tallest of the bunch steps forward and goes muzzle-to-muzzle with the vizier.

"Traitor!" cries the big dragon. "You turned on our queen. Saita lies dead and yet? You seek your own selfish gain."

"Dragon scum," counters the vizier.

"I've endured your insults long enough," counters the ice dragon. He takes in a long and rattling breath. I've seen this move before. When the dragon exhales, he'll release a shower of ice.

And I stand right in the dragon's line of chilly-n-nasty spew. I could run, but we zombie types don't really do that too well.

Dare lets out an inhuman roar. Everyone falls deadly silent. "Stop this now. Calla has work to do." He gestures to me. "Whenever you're ready, my love."

"Thank you."

I grip the sword hilt more tightly. This is what you call a high-pressure moment. Fire drakes and ice dragons loom all around. Not to mention the presence of my hulked-out boyfriend. There's extra pressure in having so many eyes on me.

Yet I push those thoughts aside. There's been too much life lost today. Now it's time for healing. I focus my energy on the Ogham sword in my grasp. The ley magic within speaks to me. Just like back in the ley castle with Dare, I know exactly what must happen next.

And that's to jam the *business end* of the Ogham sword directly into the ground while speaking the incantation. So that's what I do.

One for many,
Magic of plenty.
Take back your power; make me life!

As I speak the words, I picture the ley magic within the sword rejoining the same energy within the earth.

For a moment, nothing happens.

Then blue light surrounds Saita. Muscles rebuild on her bones. Skin and clothes follow next. Dare's mother moves to stand once more.

Blue light shines around me as well. Energy and life pulse back into me. My body becomes healed and whole again. For his part, Dare goes back to being his regular dimensions. Not sure how I feel about that. I was a little interested in figuring out this secret half of his.

Saita gets right to it. She marches over the vizier while screeching the words, "How dare you?" The two yell back and forth. Nice to see Saita ticked off at someone else for a change.

For days now, bands of worry have been slowly tightening around my chest. Now those constrictions loosen for the first time in what feels like ages.

This is good. It's over.

Only it's not.

The Ogham sword slips from my grasp. Little by little, it sinks into the earth. The ground rumbles violently, forcing me to shift my weight from side to side in an effort to stay upright. Plumes of blue smoke spit out from nearby mountain peaks.

Every inch of my body goes on alert as I realize the truth. All that new ley magic I just pumped into the ground? Now it's overloading the whole region.

Boom! Boom! Boom!

One by one, all the peaks of Hyperborea explode into very angry volcanoes of death.

Crap.

Hyperborea

Boom! Boom! Boom!

There's no need for a big public service announcement here. Everyone knows it's time to flee. Ice dragons retake to the skies. Fire drakes run back into the forest… and those guys can really book when they set their minds to it.

I open a ley door. Together with Dare, I help anyone without serious wings to escape, and that includes Jolly, Oinky, Bilge, and my parents.

At last, it's just me, Dare, and the perfect time to skedaddle. Two last stragglers step out from the woods. I wave in their direction. "Over here! We can help!"

The pair move past the plumes of ash and smoke. At last, their identities are clear.

It's the Usurper and Guinevere, and they've decided to team up.

You've got to be kidding me.

I bring these two back to life with the Ogham sword... and this is their plan? Sheesh. Good thing Dare brought lots of extra swords and my fae magic is back.

Screw these guys.

Dare leaps high with his longsword gripped firmly. The blade slices the Usurper in half from head to toe. That guy's not coming back again.

Speaking of people who shouldn't be here, Guinevere has looked better. The ley magic managed to get her head back on, but it isn't really straight. This gives her the impression that she's looking at me out of her left eye.

And it means she's now the owner of some really terrible spatial awareness.

I hold up my hands, palms forward. "Last chance, Guinevere. You can still choose a different path. Be more like your brother instead of only avenging him."

"Never!"

With that, Guinevere steps *smack dab* into one of the many freshly-made mini potholes currently marking the clearing. And for these new pits, I can thank my new friends, the supervolcanoes.

Guinevere trips and falls over. Without getting too

graphic, let's just say she's headless again. I'd feel badly for her, but it's been a big day and she tried to kill me twice. Plus, Dare and I still need to get out of here.

Hiss! Hiss!

Geysers of liquid blue magic erupt all around us. Dare turns to me. "We must leave. Now."

I scan for the last ley door I made. Those usually stay put for a little while. Unfortunately, with all this crazy magic around, everything I built has disappeared.

Time for Plan B.

Kneeling down, I reach for another ley line inside the earth. Minutes slowly pass, which isn't a fun experience. The ley geysers are getting rowdy. More smoke appears than ever before.

Finally, my fingers brush a ley line. I grasp it with all my strength and pull. Hard. At first, it doesn't budge.

Thankfully, Dare sees what's wrong and doesn't wait for an invitation. The prince places his hands atop mine, Working together, we pull up the ley line and make our final escape door.

As we step back into my bedroom, I some to another major realization. That adventure was a total pain.

But Dare and I did find treasure in the end.

- Calla

Dear Diary,

The last few weeks have been a total blur. Saita came by the summer palace and apologized. She said the stress of the Usurper was too much to handle. I was something she could focus on... and she got carried away. She asked me to forgive her, and I think she really meant it.

So I have forgiven her.

Although I'll keep one eye on Saita, just in case her stress levels spike up again.

Ivy and Vadin are back together. Turns out, Vadin told his parents he likes Ivy and doesn't care about titles. They're both hanging out at the Mermaid Retreat and loving it.

There's an unexpected bonus to making Ivy a noble.

It's made the rest of the court nervous that I'll demote them all and have my friends take their places. And it's an idea at that. Although the nobility are trying to play more nicely—by showing up to court, for instance—so we'll see how that goes.

Jolly is back on his regular spot, along with Poppa and Muti. Bilge and Oinky are now spending time putting away all the cauldrons and storage barrels from his potion master's study. It seems Guinevere promised she'd take the healing potion if needed, just like her brother. Bilge brewed all that stuff for nothing.

Guinevere was a good liar.

Most of my time has been spent planning a new announcement for my decrees. My birth parents have been super helpful. Turns out, they'd been pulling ley lines for days, trying to figure out how to best aid me. And in the end, that was not to do anything at all.

I could've spent years learning about ley elemental magic and I might never tap into the power of the Ogham sword. By rescuing Dare in the ley pit, I caught up quickly on some necessary skills. So in the end, my parents are pretty awesome.

Everyone's been pitching in on ways to help the changelings. It'll be an investment and a process. But it's a start. That's what counts.

What did Dare say? *It's not how you fall, it's how you get back up.* I'm standing.

Which brings me to the big news for today. I'm back in my royal courtroom and the place is packed. There are representatives here from all levels of fae society, as well as some changelings. Folks aren't holding hands or anything. Still, it's my first official decree announcement to all my people. That's worth celebrating.

I stand before my flowery throne. Both sets of parents wait nearby, along with Saita, Bilge, Oinky, and Ivy. Dare is right at my side, which is only fitting. If it hadn't been for the prince's encouragement, I wouldn't be here.

I lift my scepter. The room falls silent.

"Greetings, everyone. I am Queen Calla, and we're gathered here to celebrate the first of two major changes that will bring more justice to the summer realm."

Here I pause for dramatic effect. Everyone seems engaged. That's good.

"For ages, fae have stolen humans away from earth. This practice is wrong. The winter realm stopped doing this decades ago. It's beyond time that the summer realm did the same."

Next, I raise my first scroll of parchment and show it to the crowd. "This decree allowed all changelings to walk away from their so-called owners. No magical bindings. No reprisals. I have since created a new land for our changeling brethren to recover while they decide what they want to do next, whether it's return to Earth or stay here in Faerie as independent citizens. Those borders will be guarded by my best soldiers. All changelings will be safe and protected."

I lift the second decree. "Ages ago, the High Council was for everyone. Then Lazare changed to the Elven High Council. We rulers need a council that represents everyone. It's the best way for us to find out what our subjects really think. And our people are more than just elves. With this decree, I removed Lazare's decree and sent out new invitations to a wider group of fae. And since I know there might be some fears about joining, I'll visit each proposed council member personally to explain my plans."

I set the decrees aside and face the group again. That was a lot of formal stuff. Just as I could sense what the ley magic wanted, I can feel what my subjects need now. And that's something real from me.

"Look," I begin. "I know I'm young and have a wild reputation. I *will* make mistakes. But I also have some of the best folks in Faerie at my back. And more than that, I will work my hardest for each of you, every day. I know you'll need time to believe that. All I ask is for you to give me a chance to prove it."

I shrug. "That's it. I don't have anything else to add. Thank you for coming here today."

I retake my seat on the throne. The room stays silent. Panic streams through my limbs.

This is a mistake. I can't do this.

The crowd breaks out into a cheer. There are cries of "All hail, Queen Calla." I let out a long breath.

It worked. So far.

The crowd calls for another speech. I stand back up, smile, and tell them everything I plan to do.

Dare & Me

I explain my plans for a long time. It seems all those years I complained about every little thing in Faerie turned out to be useful research.

After an hour, I thank everyone again and retreat to my dining hall. There's more celebrating here with friends and family.

The royal orchestra begins to play. Dare and I step out onto the dance floor. It strikes me that this moment is just like my nightmare from some weeks ago. Only while that experience was awful, this one is perfect.

For the first song, it's traditional for the top royal to own the dance floor. So it's just me and Dare for now. The prince leans in and whispers in my ear.

"Your Changeling-Council Plan is off to a great start," he says.

"All three parts."

Dare kisses the top of my year. "What's this new addition?"

"It's always been there. Number three is Calla and Dare."

"Anything more specific?"

"Not yet. We've got time."

"That we do."

And the prince spins me about until I laugh. In this moment, I know a single truth more deeply than ever before. I never had to have three things on my list.

Sometimes, all you need is one person.

- Calla

—The End—

The adventure continues in Winter Prince, Pixieland Diaries
Book 4

There's good and bad news for our favorite pixie, Calla. First, the plus side. After lifetime of crushing, Calla's finally dating the elf Prince, Dare. SUH-weet.

Second, the not-so-great stuff. Dare has a maniacal brother, Reiver, who's supposedly dead. Only he's not. Reiver is very much alive and causing mega-trouble in the frozen lands of Faerie.

Time for Calla and Dare to face the Winter Prince.

Pixieland Diaries Series

1. Pixieland Diaries

2. Calla

3. Dare

4. Winter Prince

5. Ley Queen

THE CITIZENS OF ERRIGAL

After my trip to the Talking Desert, some Errigal folks visited me at the summer palace. I drew images of these super-cool visitors! Check them out on the pages ahead...

PS. *These images are only available in this special enhanced edition because sometimes, we all need secret cool stuff.*

Boo

Foo

Cobza

Dame Branch

Laughing Dragon

ALSO BY CHRISTINA BAUER

Check out ANGELBOUND, the kick-ass paranormal romance! Read on for a sample…

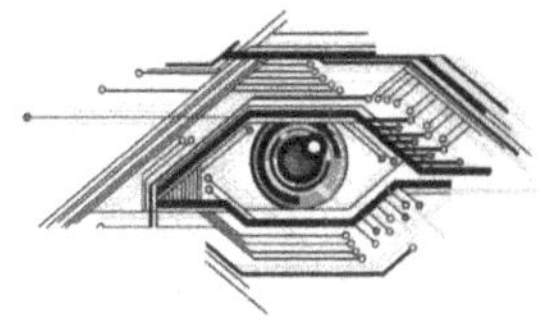

A kick-ass heroine + a swoon-worthy prince + an all-girl heist = SCYTHE!!!

STANDARD APPENDIX OF COOL STUFF

7. Fairies and Frosting

8. Towers and Tithes

9. Evil Queens and Goblin Kings

Angelbound Origins

About a quasi (part demon and part human) girl who loves kicking butt in Purgatory's Arena

1. Angelbound

2. Scala

3. Acca

4. Thrax

5. The Dark Lands

6. The Brutal Time

7. Armageddon

8. Quasi Redux

9. Clockwork Igni

10. Lady Reaper

11. Angry Gods

12. Phantom Corsair

Angelbound Lincoln

The Angelbound experience as told by Prince Lincoln

1. Duty Bound

2. Lincoln

3. Trickster

4. Baculum

5. Angelfire

6. Rixa

7. Mordred

Angelbound Offspring

The next generation takes on Heaven, Hell, and everything in between

1. Maxon

2. Portia

3. Zinnia

4. Rhodes

5. Kaps

6. Mack

7. Huntress

** This is a completed series.*

Angelbound Xavier

Xavier's story

1. Archenemy

2. Archnemesis

3. Archangel

Dimension Drift

Dystopian adventures with science, snark, and hot aliens

1. Scythe

2. Umbra

3. Alien Minds

4. ECHO Academy

This is a completed series.

Beholder

Where a medieval farm girl discovers necromancy and true love

1. Cursed

2. Concealed

3. Cherished

4. Crowned

5. Cradled

This is a completed series.

ACKNOWLEDGMENTS

If you're reading my freaking acknowledgements, chances are, I should thank you for something. So, for the record: you are awesome, dear reader.

That said, huge and heartfelt thanks must go out to my husband and son for their rock-solid support. Being an author means a lot of early mornings, late nights, long weekends, and never-ending patience. You two are the best guys in the universe, period.

After that, I must thank the extensive network of reviewers, friends and colleagues who helped me build my writing chops in general. Gracias.

Finally, deep affection goes out to my late, much loved, and dearly missed Aunt Sandy and Uncle Henry. You saw the writer in me, always. Thank you, first and last.

Christina Bauer thinks that fantasy books are like bacon: they just make life better. All of which is why she writes romance novels that feature demons, dragons, wizards, witches, elves, elementals, and a bunch of random stuff that she brainstorms while riding the Boston T. Oh, and she includes lots of humor and kick-ass chicks, too. Christina lives in Newton, MA with her husband, son, and semi-insane golden retriever, Ruby.

Stalk Christina on Social Media

Blog:
http://monsterhousebooks.com/blog/
category/christina

Facebook:
https://www.facebook.com/authorBauer/

Instagram:
https://www.instagram.com/christina_cb_bauer/

Twitter:
@CB_Bauer

VLOG:
https://tinyurl.com/Vlogbauer

Web site:
www.bauersbooks.com

BONUS APPENDIX OF GOODIES

*L*et's say you don't know me too well. You might see me parked in your favorite Starbucks. Perhaps you've spied me talking to myself while I write on my laptop. Even so, no matter who you may be, chances are when you first meet me, you'll say: "Hey, you're the girl with the big red backpack."

And, yes. Yes, I am.

Let me explain. I write a crap-ton of books. Right now, I'm averaging four full novels each year, which is pretty crazy. I also juggle being a Mom and having a day job, so I must be ready to write at a moment's notice. To accomplish this, my backpack has all the essentials:

MacBook Air. I can drag this around without snapping my spine. I wasn't always this lucky. Some of my previous laptops could have crushed diamonds. No lie.

Bose Noise-Cancelling Headphones. These are essential because inevitably, I must write somewhere that noisy, like a coffee shop or airport. I'm really sensitive to sound, so the headphones are key.

Writing Glasses. I have two sets so glasses: my 'wear these so I don't fall down the stairs' variety and my reading ones. If I want to write without getting a migraine, I must use the former.

Other Electronics. I also drag around my cell phone, miscellaneous chargers and wires, my Kindle (because maybe I'll get a chance to read, who knows?) and sundry pens (sometimes I'm asked to sign stuff.)

So that's it: the secret contents of my backpack. Whenever I tell folks that's what I carry around, I think it's a little disappointing for them. I'm guessing people are pulling for something cooler or more dramatic, like a magic trick or human head. Every so often, I toy with the idea of putting something more creative in there, but I toss the concept aside. The stuff in my head is crazy enough, and that needs the laptop to come out :)

And speaking of my backpack, it's time for me to get back to writing! Thanks for taking the time to read about the crap I drag around with me.

For anyone who's interested, here's how I write my stuff…

Step One. I create a series treatment.

By this, I mean the overall direction for a series. Across five books, what happens to the heroine? Does she get married, become a queen, what? In college I learned to write for film, so I feel comfortable following a screenwriting model for story development. A treatment (to me anyway) is a two-page summary of what the series will be about. The end product will deviate from this plan, but *meh*. A nice overview of treatments can be found here.

Step Two. I outline my book.

Here I use a film writing format called SAVE THE CAT in which you outline everything into three acts. An overview of SAVE THE CAT can be found here, along with examples and downloads.

Step Three. I create Pinterest Boards.

Next I create Pinterest inspiration boards for each key character and setting. As of writing this, I have hundreds of boards and thousands of pins.

Step Four. I paste my outline into Scrivener

This is a writing tool where each chapter becomes a file folder that you can easily move around. Once my flow is pretty solid, I move my story onto yet another way of looking at story structure...

Step Five. I load my chapter list into Excel

In my work, I often have complex and overlapping story lines. To make sure I'm focusing on what's important, I map my chapters into Excel and cross-reference that against key themes. And now, with all that behind me, I get to the actual writing of the book!

Step Six. I write chapter one

Please note that I do not start to write in earnest until *all the stuff above* is complete. Early on in my career, I used to have writer's block ... or I'd write ten chapters and chuck nine of them. Now that rarely happens, but it's because I've found that all my prep work is key. Everyone's process is different, but there you go.

Step Seven. I perfect each chapter, read for flow, and a ton of other stuff

Once the structure of a story is set, each chapter is its own mini structure (in my writing anyway.)

Step Eight. It all goes into a series bible

Each series has a bible (fancy name for a long word doc) where I keep a list of characters and descriptions.

So that's it: My writing process in eight steps.

Here's the sordid tale of my (admittedly failed) experience with turning my work into a TV series..

Getting "The Call"

I've had a number of folks reach out to me about turning my stuff into a movie or TV show. The closest I got was when a producer wanted to turn my novels, The Fairy Tales of the Magicorum, into a streaming series. The producers and I had some calls, we met for lunch, and then they asked me to write a script *on spec* (which means for free.) I have no track record in Hollywood, so that's what I did.

Sales Process

Before becoming a full-time author, I worked in sales and marketing in many different industries. No matter what the area, it all comes down to a matter of numbers. Only a small percentage of opportunities turn into anything. So I didn't want to get too cranked up about this. Still, the fact that I was asked for a script was a good sign. Also, we got into some details, too. The producer talked about my joining the writing team if the series got picked up. So I started to do some research.

And I fucking panicked.

What Worried Me

One. Writing TEAM. TEAM!!! That means creating in committee. I hate this.

Two. Right now, I have control over my business. When I want to write a book, I just do it. When you're a writer in Hollywood, you're dependent on a ton of other people for your work to reach the public. And you must shepherd your writing through lots of edits that you (let's face it) probably don't agree with.

Three. You can make a lot of money. This shouldn't seem like a negative, but it kind of is. The cash distracts from items number one and two. I'm a self sufficient writer. I pay my bills and run my own show. What do I *really* get out of more money and hassle? How much is enough?

Four. If I lose control over my work, I could start to suck. Not good.

Overall, I wasn't crying in my soup when the

producer told me that the streaming service took a pass. I sighed, filed the script in a folder deep in my MacBook, and focused on my next novel. Hope my experience helps to illuminate what you may (or may not) want to do with your own writing!

10. Eat fried foods

9. Take naps

8. Drink mochas

7. Watch puppy and panda videos on YouTube

6. Ignore housework

. . .

5. Be at peace with ignoring housework. Name the dust bunnies. It helps!

4. Find a special place to be your writing spot

3. Set aside sacred writing time (early mornings or late nights work for me)

2. Stick to launch schedules

1. You have amazing stories to share that only you can bring into the world. Never give up. Trust your gift.

*H*ow do I create characters? Here are my three simple steps…

Tip #1... Pick a language base for the character

OK, so I got this one from <u>Tolkien</u>. He used the language and history of Finland in order to inspire his version of elves. In my experience, language drives so much of a character, it isn't even funny. It gives you a way to name them, the places in their lives and their history.

PRO TIP: <u>Google Translate</u> is awesome here. There are also about a million web sites for baby names by culture.

Tip #2... Make Pinterest boards for the character

I'm a super visual writer, so I start creating characters by building boards of inspirational pics. I begin with a general idea, such as the fact that the person is a ruler or whatever. Then I pull images onto my board. This takes time because I toss the stuff that doesn't fit and keep the pieces that do. In general, I delete about ten images for every one that works.

For me, it's also important to have a general Pinterest board of cool stuff that inspires me in general. I keep those boards hidden from general viewing. My public boards are here. Sarah J Maas has some cool boards that you may want to check out as well.

PRO TIP: Visit Pinterest if you haven't already.

Tip #3... Write Soliloquies

If I'm stuck on a character, I'll write a page-long soliloquy about their views on the world or whatever topic strikes me. It's important that this is just something that exists... versus having all this pressure to force it into the story.

Author Virginia Woolf says "I dig out beautiful caves behind my characters." To me, I think this means you must get comfortable with creating tons of content and backstory about a character that never appears on the page. That said, I think readers can always sense when a character has that extra level of work behind them. Not sure how they can tell, but they always do!

So that's it... some of my favorite tools and tricks. Hope you found them helpful!

J've written a ton of books. Here's what to look for in a publisher.

CAVEAT: I'm independently published, so these are my third party observations.

First Thing To Look For: Yourself

Okay, I know that sounds hokey, but it's important to know what kind of books you want to spend the rest of your life with. For example, some authors have told me that they wrote in a particular genre because it was hot and they wanted to get published. But then when they were successful, they felt trapped into doing something they really didn't like.

For me, I find it helps to think of publishers as department stores. They have their men's section, evening wear, shoes and so on. They're looking for hot trends that will pull people into their shop. If you get labeled as a great shoe designer, then it's hard to go back and restart in menswear.

Second Thing to Look For: The Editor or Agent

You know when you first get to high school and everyone is picking out their friends? It's just a great time to meet people. Along that line, you want to find editors or agents who are on the prowl for something. Back to the department store example, their CEO just said, *go find some new shoes because this line up sucks!*

There are a lot of books out there, but what I like to check is a web site called Publishers Marketplace. You see who is doing deals on what and for how much. It costs $20/month and you can sign up for one month if you like. You can also see how people are pitching their stuff. It's best to use the latest hot terms in your pitch, if that makes sense.

True confession: I read Publishers Marketplace to see what *not* to write. Deals tend to go in waves. For instance, if the big publishers are all doing mermaid books, then I want to avoid the seven seas.

So there you have it—my indie take on finding a publisher!

For them's that's curious, here are my thoughts on writing paranormal romance for young adults...

Why I Write Paranormal

To begin with, I read a lot of contemporary romance and I love-love-LOVE that genre, but when I try to write it, I get really hung up on the whole "that guy would never do that" thing. Here's a classic example of what the voice in my head says during such times: "Whoa therem Bauer! Bad boys stay bad. Unless you have this guy complete twenty years of therapy or have an anyeurysm, the dude is not going to change." So, when I start to write 100% contemporary, I end up sticking to real life. All of which brings me to my problem with writing that genre.

Real life is really freaking depressing.

Life is hard and writing is my escape. Long story short, I've found that I can make things fun if I stick to fantasy. Within this uber genre, I've tried epic-style 'swords and sorcery' stuff (my Beholder series) as well as urban fantasy (Angelbound novels). With my new book, WOLVES AND ROSES, I have come the closest ever to crafting contemporary romance. There are certainly some paranormal elements in the book, but it's not like the book is set in Purgatory or Hell like the Angelbound series (Beholder takes place in a modified version of the middle ages.) So, paranormal has been an evolution for me.

The Pros of Paranormal

I love world building and paranormal allows my imagination to run wild. I have a whole ancient Egypt thing coming with the future books after WOLVES AND ROSES which I am SUPER PSYCHED to share with you. But I can't because SPOILERS.

All in all, the great part about paranormal is that I'm not stuck with anyone's rules, even if those rules are so-called reality.

The Cons of Paranormal

In my opinion, the big challenge of paranormal is the same as its greatest benefit: world building. Let me explain. When you're writing in 'reality,' you can just say 'a guy walks into a bar' and everyone knows what you mean: the guy is a dude who is not too young or old. He's also moving forward on two feet and wearing pants. And the bar is a sort of generic place with bottles of booze and lots of tables.

Now say you step into a fairy soiree (this actually happens in my book, WOLVES AND ROSES). What do the fairies look like? Do any of them wear pants? Do they fly or walk? Where do they have celebrations anyway? In other words, I have to set a TON of stuff up without taking up two pages describing everything before I get to the actual story. Not gonna lie. This part is a pain in the ass. But if I do it right, people feel transported to another realty in the story, which is what I'm after.

PRO TIP: It's easy to get caught up in your own world building. To paraphrase Virginia Wolff: I carve out great caves behind my characters and only allow the reader to see a small sliver. You have to build a ton and pitch it. The reader will only feel that it's there and that's OK.

y Calla, Star of the Pixieland Diaries

By now, you've probably heard about the launch of my dairies, a series of books which have been proofread by the human author, Christina Bauer.

Since I am a powerful fairy and fascinating person in general, I shall now share something that isn't in these books: a description of my typical day.

My day begins when I wake up. Now, I was raised as a pixie and my kind don't like mornings. Turns out, my heritage is a little more complicated than simple pixiedom. Still, mornings can kiss my fairy butt.

Once I eventually get up, I ensure that I look fabulous. This doesn't take much time because I'm naturally gorgeous: pink hair and matching wings, curvy body, and violet eyes. I don't even have to cast a spell for my loveliness to shine forth.

After that, I hang with my adopted parents, Poppa and Muti, for a bit. My parents are tree sprites who come to about ankle height on yours truly. They've got silver hair and matching robes as well as… wait for it… all their teeth. That's a big deal when you're forty thousand years old.

Next I fly over to the Pixieland Citadel to hang with my friend Bilge the hobgoblin. Although Bilge is an expert in brewing potions, his organizational skills suck. On a typical day, I might help him shelve his little vials of magical goodness.

All this time, I do not obsess about my best friend, Prince Dare. I don't think about how cute he is, what with his muscly form, long hair and intense eyes. I certainly don't obsess about Dare's next visit.

Well, there you have it! My day. Huzzah.